WE HAD LEARNED LONG BEFORE WE EVER SAW THE CARIBBEAN THAT BEAUTIFUL SCENERY PROVIDES THE MOST CHILLING BACKGROUND FOR ANY KIND OF TERRORISM.
—The Rose Diary

OVER THE COURSE OF THE YEAR WE HAD TO HIRE OVER A HUNDRED DIFFERENT PEOPLE. WE PAID OUT NEARLY $475,000 IN OVERHEAD EXPENSES . . . FORGERS, COUNTERFEITERS, GUN SALESMEN, INFORMERS, DOPE PEDDLERS, WHORES, PICKPOCKETS, AMERICAN INTELLIGENCE MEN, TOP MERCENARIES . . . AND NOT ONE OF THESE PEOPLE WAS EVER TOLD EXACTLY WHAT IT WAS THAT WE WERE PUTTING TOGETHER IN THE CARIBBEAN . . .
—The Rose Diary

WHAT WE DID IN SAN DOMINICA WAS SOMETHING LIKE TURNING LOOSE CHARLES STARKWEATHER AND CARIL FUGATE, SPECK, BREMER, MANSON AND SQUEAKY FROMME ALL IN THE SAME PLACE AT THE SAME TIME.
—The Rose Diary

Also by James Patterson
available now from Ballantine Books:

THE THOMAS BERRYMAN NUMBER

The Season of the Machete

James Patterson

BALLANTINE BOOKS • NEW YORK

The Season of the Machete

April 30, 1975; Turtle Bay

On the gleaming white-sand lip of the next cove, King-fish and the Cuban can see a couple walking on the beach. Just fuzzy-gray stick figures at this distance.

Hidden in palm trees and sky-blue wild lilies, the two great and nearly famous killers watch the mystery couple disappear into the cove itself, slowly coming their way.

The Cuban is wearing a skull-tight red bandanna like Aunt Jemima; rip-kneed khaki trousers; scuffed, pale-orange, construction boots from Manny's Army-Navy Store in Miami. The man called Kingfish has on nothing but greasy U.S. Army khakis.

The overdeveloped muscles of both men ripple in the hard, beating Caribbean sun.

The bright sun makes diamonds and blinking aster-isks all over the sea. It glints off a sugar-cane machete hanging from the belt of the Cuban.

The weather-beaten farm implement is two and a half feet long, and sharp as a Gillette Blue Blade.

South of their hiding place, a great wrecked schooner —the *Isabelle Anne*—sits lonely and absurd, visited by yellow birds and fish only. Thirty yards farther south, the beach elbows around steep black rocks and makes a crystal path for walking. At this sharp bend lies: reeffish, coral, sargassum, oyster drills, sea urchins.

Soon now, the two killers expect the couple from the next cove to appear on the narrow white path.

Perhaps a dark, bejeweled prime minister up on holiday from South America? Or an American politician with his corn- and milk-fed secretary/mistress?

Someone worth their considerable fees and passage to this serene and beautiful part of the world. Someone worth $35,000 apiece for less than one week's work.

Instead, a pretty pair of adolescents turn the seaweed-strewn corner into Turtle Bay.

A bony, long-haired rich boy. A white-blonde girl in a Club Méditerranée T-shirt.

They clumsily get out of their shirts, shorts, sandals, and underwear on the run. They shout something about rotten eggs going last, and run into the low, starry waves, balls and little tits naked.

Twenty or thirty feet over their heads, laughing sea gulls make a sound almost like mountain sheep bleating.

Aaaaaa! Aaaaaa! Aaaaaa! Aaaaaa!

The man called Kingfish puts out an expensive black cigar in the sand. A low, animal moan rises up out of his throat.

"We couldn't have come all this way to kill these two children."

The Cuban cautions him. "Wait and see."

"Aaagghh! Aaagghh!" The young hippie boy offers tin-ear bird imitations from the rippling water.

The blonde girl screams. "I can't stand it. It's so goddamn unbelievably beautiful!"

She dives into starry, aquamarine waves. Surfaces with her long hair plastered down like grease. Her

2

white breasts are small, nubby, up-pointed and rubbery from the cool water.

"I love this place already. Don't *ever* want to go back. Gramercy Park—*yeck!* I spit on East Twenty-third Street. Yeck! Yahoo! Yow!"

The Cuban slowly raises his hand above the blue lilies and prickle bushes. He waves in the direction of a green sedan parked on a lush hill overlooking the beach.

The sedan's horn sounds once. The signal.

Unbelievably, this *is* the beginning.

An eerie silence comes over the place.

Heartbeats, surf, little else.

The boy and girl lay on fluffy beach towels to dry under the sun. They close their eyes and see spirals and kaleidoscopes on the backs of their eyelids.

The girl sings, " 'Eastern's got my sunshine. . . .' "

The boy makes an impolite gurgling sound.

As the girl opens one eye, she feels a hard slap on the top of her hair. Her whole head is painfully hot all of a sudden and she feels dizzy. She starts to say *Aahhh,* and chokes on thick, bubbling blood instead.

Pop . . . pop . . .

The slightest rifle cracks echo in the surrounding hills.

Bullets travel out of an expensive West German rifle at 3,300 feet per second.

Then Kingfish and the Cuban come and stand over the bodies, over the lightly blood-spotted towels. Kingfish touches the boy's cheek and produces an unexpected moan, almost a growl.

"I don't think I like Mr. Damian Rose," he says in a surprisingly soft, French-accented voice. "Very sorry I left Paris now. He's let this one live."

The dying nineteen-year-old coughs. Blue eyes rolling, he speaks. "Why?" the boy asks. "Didn't do anything. . . ."

The Cuban swings the sugar-cane machete, high. He chops down as if he's in the thickest possible jungle brush, as if he's cutting a tree.

Chop, wriggle, lift.

Chop, wriggle, lift.

The expensive killer meticulously attacks both bodies with the long broadsword. Clean, hard strokes. Devastating.

Blood red as paint squirts and sprays as high as the man himself. Flesh and bone part like butter in the path of the razor-sharp knife. Puddles of frothy blood are quickly soaked up by the sand, leaving dark-red stains.

When the butchering is over, the Cuban drives the machete deep into the sand. He carefully sets a red Rude Boy's wool hat over the knife's handle and hasp.

Then both killers look up into the hills. They see the distant figure of Damian Rose beside the shiny green car. They can see that the handsome blond man is waving for them to come back. Waving his fancy German rifle high over his head.

What they can't see is that Damian Rose is smiling.

The Preface

The Damian and Carrie Rose Diary

Consider the raw power and potential of the good old-fashioned thrill kill. Under proper supervision, of course.

The Rose Diary

January 23, 1976; New York City

At 6:30 A.M. on the twenty-third of January, the birth date of his only child, Mary Ellen, Bernard Siegel— tall, dark, slightly myopic—begins his "usual" loose scrambled eggs, poppy-seed bagel, and black coffee breakfast at Wolf's Delicatessen on West 57th Street in New York City.

After the satisfying meal, Siegel takes a Checker cab through slushy, brown snow to 800 Third Avenue. He uses his private collection of seven keys to let himself into the modern dark-glass building, then into the offices of the publisher *par excellence* for whom he works, and finally into the largest *small* office on that floor—his office—to try and get some busywork done before the many-too-many phones begin to ring; to try and get home early enough to spend some time with his daughter. On her twelfth birthday.

An uninvited young woman, very, very tan, squeaky clean, with premature silver all through her long, sandy hair, is sitting on the editor's couch.

The woman is watching either 777 Third Avenue (the building across and down Third Avenue); her own reflection off the dark, double-glazed windows; or Siegel himself.

Bernard Siegel says, "One—who the hell are you? Two—I don't really care. Three—please leave."

"My name is Carrie Rose." The woman turns full-face toward him. She looks to be twenty-eight or twenty-nine; spectacularly poised and cool, if nothing else.

"I've come to make you an even more famous man than you are now. You are Siegel, aren't you?"

The editor can't hold back a slight smile. The smallest possible parting of thin, severe lips. She calls him *Siegel.*

But damn these shameless, impudent young writers, he's thinking at the same time. Has she actually *slept* in his office to get an interview? To give lucky him first crack at this year's *Fear of Flying;* or *Flying;* or *The Flies.*

Squinting badly, pathetically, for a man under forty, Siegel studies Carrie Rose. *Mrs.* Carrie Rose, he's to find out soon. Wife of Damian Rose. Soldier-of-fortune herself.

Under closer scrutiny, the young woman is first of all striking; then tall; then fashionably trim. *Vogue*-ish.

For the interview, she has on large tortoise-shell eye-glasses that make her look more sharp-witted than she probably is; plus a blue pin-striped jacket and skirt—to keep Siegel off his guard, he's sure. An old Indian dodge.

"All right, I'm Siegel," the near-sighted editor finally admits. "I'm hardly famous. And this sort of clever, gratuitous nonsense doesn't cut it with me. . . . Please leave my office. Go back and write one more draft of your wonderful book. Make a regular-hours appointment with my—"

"Oh, but you are famous, Bernard." The woman interrupts him with an ingénue's toothy grin. "You're so well known, in fact, that busy people like myself go to great inconvenience to *give* you million-dollar book properties. Books that will make, at the very least, *dents* in history."

Now Siegel actually laughs. A little cruel, but she deserves it.

"Only a million for it?"

Carrie Rose laughs too. "Something like that."

She examines Siegel closely. Looks around his office —unmatched oak and pine bookcases on two of the walls. An Olivetti Lettera typewriter tucked inside a banged-up roll-top desk. Sheafs of crisp white bond; new, shiny book jackets pinned to a cork board; manuscripts in different-color typewriter-paper boxes.

The editor.

Siegel sets his briefcase on his desk, kicks off his loafers, goes to start a pot of Mr. Coffee.

"Well, where is the magnum opus?" he asks.

"Why, you haven't had it ghost-written yet," the young woman on the couch says. *Carrie Rose.*

"Your writer's source material will be a diary my husband, Damian, and I kept last year. An unusual, very original diary that will cost you *two* million dollars. It's about . . . an awful nest of machete murders. Over a hundred of them."

The pretty woman says it so cool. . . . *An awful nest of machete murders.*

9

Part I

The Season of the Machete

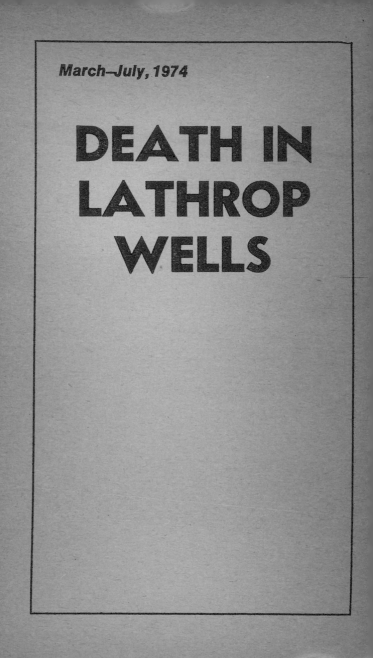

March—July, 1974

DEATH IN LATHROP WELLS

Damian theorizes that within fifty years man will move onto and into the sea. San Dominica is only a very small beginning. An exploratory expedition. Kid stuff. The people who engineered it don't understand their own inner motivations . . . 3/5ths of the world is water, and that is about to be fought over on a staggering scale. . . .

The Rose Diary

February 24, 1974; Lathrop Wells, Nevada

As the stupid, piggy Chevrolet Impala floats through buzzard-infested desert, Isadore "the Mensch" Goldman is thinking that he's slightly surprised there really is a *state* of Nevada.

Every so often, though, the Chevrolet passes a tin road sign with PROPERTY OF THE STATE OF NEVADA stamped into it by some poor convict at Washoe County Jail.

Once, Goldman even spots some Nevadans: a woman and small children with frayed ankle boots, turquoise jewelry, faces the color of pretzel sticks.

Somewhere out here they tested H-bombs, the old man is thinking. At Mercury, Nevada.

Then the seventy-four-year-old's mind goes walking. He remembers something itchy about the still-not-to-be-believed Bay of Pigs invasion. Then a very brief, fuzzy association he'd had with Rafael Trujillo that same year: 1961.

Goldman's *History*. All leading up to February 24, 1974. The biggest day of the old man's life.

Maybe.

A man named Vincent "Zio" Tuch is patting Isadore's gray-striped banker's trousers at one baggy knee.

Death spots are all over Tuch's unsteady hand.

"Bizee Izzee, what are you thinkin'?" Tuch rasps. "You thinkin' this is a big old-fashioned setup, Izzie? That's what I'm thinkin'."

"Aahh . . . I'm getting too damn old to think all the time." The *consigliere* casually dismisses the powerful old *capo*. It is a typically stupid, if well-meant, Mustache Pete question.

Old Tuch tells him to go make shit in his own pants —which is also typical.

Also typical is the fact that the *caporegime* smells of Wildroot Creme Oil spilled over twenty-year-old dandruff.

Goldman had flatly predicted that the final meeting at Lathrop Wells would be ridiculous beyond human belief.

Even he is surprised at the *consistency* of the silly putty, however.

It looks like the opening scene of an Alfred Hitchcock movie.

To begin with, both sides arrive at the farm in the most absurd "anonymous-looking" automobiles.

Goldman watches and counts bodies through the green-tinted windows of his own Impala.

There are nine chauffeurs driving such cars as Mustangs, Wildcats, Hornets, Cougars—even a Volkswagen Beetle.

There are seven out-and-out Buster Crabbe body-guard types.

Eleven actual participants besides himself and the shriveling zombie Tuch.

Somebody had remarked at the last meeting that they didn't want to have another Appalachia at Lathrop Wells: twenty Cadillac Fleetwoods suddenly arriving at some old deserted farmhouse. Drawing attention from locals or the state police.

So there are none of the usual big, black cars at the meeting in the Nevada desert.

All of the twenty-seven men wear dark business suits with the exception of one Gucci-Pucci fag and Frankie "the Cat" Rao of Brooklyn, New York.

Rao wears a black-and-white-checked sports jacket, a sleazy open-necked electric-blue shirt, white Bing Crosby shoes.

"Dirty azzhole," old Tuch says. "Azzhole with all of his pinky rings."

"All very predictable," Isadore Goldman mutters.

The old man lights up his first cigarette in over eight months. Then he heads inside through hot, heavy air that smells like horses.

Inside the farmhouse it's air-conditioned, thank God.

A Fedders is blowing dust and what looks like cereal flakes all around the rustic, low-ceilinged rooms.

Goldman notices the other side's head man whisper something to a younger man—his aide-de-camp. The younger man looks a little like the Hollywood actor Montgomery Clift.

He's named Brooks Campbell, and he'll be going to the Caribbean for them.

The older man, their side's main spokesman, is Harold Hill. Harry the Hack to the trade.

Harold Hill has spent nearly ten years in Southeast Asia, and he has a certain inscrutable look about him. Something intangible. Isadore Goldman suspects that Hill is a pretty good killer for such an obvious loser type.

Within ten minutes' time, the thirteen important negotiators have settled down comfortably around a wide beam table in the living room. Characteristically, both sides have taken opposite sides at the big wooden table.

Dark, slightly European-looking men on one side.

All-American football-player types on the other.

"By way of a brief introduction"—Goldman begins the meeting after allowing just a snitch of small talk— "it was agreed at the last meeting—January seventeenth —that if Damian and Carrie Rose were available, they would be satisfactory contract operators for everybody concerned. . . ."

Goldman peeks over his silver-rimmed spectacles. So far, no objections.

"Consequently," he goes on, "the Roses were contacted at a hotel in Paris. The St. Louis, it's called. An old gun-sellers' hangout through several wars now.

"The Roses were given one month to prepare an outline for a plan that would achieve results agreeable to both sides at this table. They declined making an appearance at this meeting, however."

The *consigliere* looks up again.

He then begins to read aloud from twenty-odd pages sent to him by the Roses. The pages outline *two* rough plans for the proposed operations. One plan is titled "Systematic Government Assassinations"; the other is simply called "Machete."

Also included in the brief is a list of pros and cons for each plan.

In fact, what seems to impress both sides gathered around the farmhouse table—what has impressed Goldman himself—is the seriousness with which both theoretical plans have been approached and researched.

They are specifically referred to as "rough," *"experimental,"* but the outline for each seems unnecessarily complete. The plans are almost obsessively airtight. Typically *Damian Rose*.

"The final bid they put in for this work," Isadore Goldman reports, "is one point two million. I myself think it's a fair estimate. I think it's low, in fact. . . .

I also think this man Damian Rose is a genius. Perhaps the woman is too. Gentlemen?"

Predictably, Frankie Rao has the first word on the plans.

"Is that fucking francs or dollars, Izzie?" he shouts down the wooden plank table. "It's fucking dollars those loonie tunes are talking about, isn't it?"

Goldman notices that their man, Harold Hill, seems startled and upset by the New York mobster.

The young man who looks like Montgomery Clift breaks into a toothpaste smile, however. *Brooks Campbell* . . . Good for you, Isadore Goldman thinks. Smart boy. Break the goddamn tensions down a little.

For the first time then, most of the men at the long wooden table laugh. Both sides laugh like hell. Even Frankie Rao begins to howl.

As the laughter dies down, Goldman nods to a dark-haired man sitting very quietly at the far end of the table.

Goldman then nods at their side's chief man, Harold Hill.

"Does the figure include all expenses?" is Hill's only question. The young man at his side, Campbell, nods as if this is his question too.

"It includes every expense," Isadore Goldman says. "The Roses expect this to take approximately one year to carry out. They'll have to use twenty to thirty other professionals along the way. A Who's Who of the most elite mercenaries."

"Dirt cheap." The quiet, dark-haired man suddenly speaks in a deep, Senate-floor voice. This man is Charles Forlenza, forty-three-year-old don of the Forlenza Family. *The boss of bosses.*

"You've gotten us a good price and good people, Isadore. As I expected . . . I can't speak for Mr. Hill, but I'm pleased with this work myself."

"The price is appropriate for this kind of guerrilla operation." Harold Hill addresses the don. "The Roses' reputation for this sort of complex, delicate work is excellent. I'm happy. Good."

At this point then, February 24, 1974, the United States, through a proprietary company called Great Western Air Transport, enters into one of the more interesting alliances in its two-hundred-year history: a large-scale working agreement with the Charles Forlenza Family of the West Coast. The Cosa Nostra.

For both sides, it means that they can immediately farm out some very necessary dirty work.

Neither the Forlenzas, nor the United States, wants to soil its hands with what has to be done in the Caribbean during 1975.

That's why they have so very carefully sought out Damian and Carrie Rose. *Les Déments*, as the couple was once called in Southeast Asia. *The Maniacs*.

Two hours after the meeting in southwestern Nevada —on the way back to Las Vegas—a silver-gray Buick Wildcat stops along a long stretch of flat, open highway.

The youthful chauffeur of the car gets out. He goes to the back door of the sedan and opens it.

Then Melo Russo politely asks his boss to get out of the car.

"Who the fuck do you think you're talking to?" Frankie Rao says to his driver—a skinny young shark in reflector sunglasses.

"All right, so fuck you, then," Melo says.

He fires three times into the back seat of the Buick. Blood flies up all over the rear windows and ceiling, then mists down onto the light-silver seat covers. Then Russo drags Frankie the Cat's body outside and puts it in the Wildcat's trunk.

It has been quietly decided at the farmhouse meeting that Frankie Rao is an unacceptable risk for Harold

Hill and the nice young man who looks like Montgomery Clift.

"Typical," Isadore Goldman mutters somewhere out on the Nevada desert.

Once—in France, this was—in June or July—
Damian had gone on a tirade about how perfect
our work in Cambodia and Vietnam had been.
How it bothered the hell out of him that no one
could know. That there was no way to capitalize
on the work . . . *Funny quirk (twist)*: In a French
village named Grasse, we sit in an espresso
house. Damian converses in English with a very
polite street-cleaner who speaks no English at all.
He tells the man every last detail about the Caribbean adventure. *"Genie! Demon! Non?"* he says
in French at the end of it. The poor, confused
street-cleaner smiles as if Damian is an insane
little boy. . . .

The Rose Diary

June 11, 1974; Paris

Three months after the Nevada meeting, in the fashionable St.-Germain section of Paris, Damian Rose swings
back and forth on a rope hammock from Printemps.

The hammock is tied onto a heavy stonework terrace.

The large, pigeon-gray terrace overlooks the Jardins
des Tuileries, the Seine, the Louvre. The scenery of
Paris is pretty as a Seurat this hazy morning.

Lying there in the late-spring sun, Rose indulges himself in his one fatuous addiction: the reading of sensationalist newspapers and magazines.

After perusing *Midnight,* then glancing at the opening stories in the *Enquirer,* the overseas edition of *Time, Soldier of Fortune* magazine, the elegant man rolls out of the hammock.

Inside his and Carrie's apartment, he gets out of a lamb's wool pullover and expensive cream gabardines. Then he starts to piece together the international costume of American students abroad.

He puts on faded denim jeans, a police-blue work shirt, lop-heeled Frye boots, and, finally, a red cowboy neckerchief. He applies light make-up to his eyes. Fits a long, dark wig over his own shorter hair.

Today, Damian Rose is playing the part of a professor from the Sorbonne.

He has to buy a small supply of drugs in Les Halles: amphetamines, cocaine, Thai sticks. Then off to meet with a mercenary soldier who calls himself the Cuban.

Tucking the work shirt tightly into jockey shorts, zipping up his jeans, Damian walks through a living room overflowing with Broadway and Haymarket Square theater paraphernalia.

Out the apartment's front door with a bang.

"Bonjour" to an old *emmerdeuse* named Marie, an ancient woman always reading newspapers in the light of the hallway window.

Then boots clomping down marble stairs to a circular courtyard inside the building itself.

Damian climbs into a small black convertible in the courtyard. He leaves the convertible's top up. Windows partially up. Visors down. He puts on blue Air Force–style sunglasses.

The sports car rolls out of the yard's black ironwork gates and Rose starts to hum an old song he likes very much—sweet "Lili Marlene."

It's a brilliantly clear and warm spring day now. White as paper. Just a little vague and fuzzy at the edges.

The sweet smell of French bread cooking fills the air on the narrow side streets.

As the shiny black car turns onto the Boulevard St.-Germain, a bicyclist—a healthy-looking girl in an oatmeal tank top—strains her long swan's neck to see the face of the young man behind the sun-dappled windshield.

The pretty Frog isn't quite fast enough, though.

No one ever has been, it seems.

As of June, 1974, no one knows what the face of Damian Rose looks like.

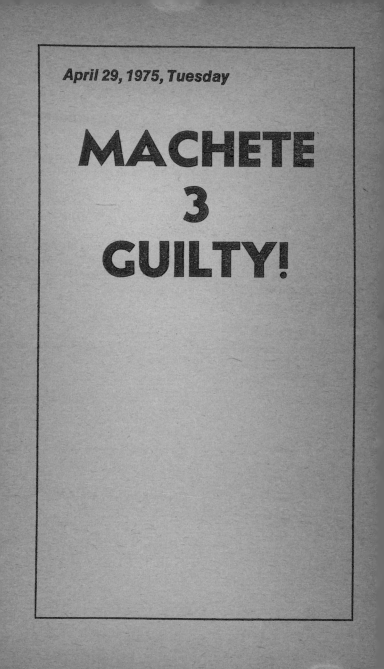

April 29, 1975, Tuesday

MACHETE
3
GUILTY!

Bookkeeping . . . Over the course of the year, we had to hire over a hundred different people. We paid out nearly $475,000 in overhead expenses. We paid forgers from Brussels, counterfeiters, gun salesmen from East Germany and the United States, informers, dope peddlers, whores, pickpockets, American Intelligence men, top mercenaries like Kingfish Toone, Blinkie Tomas (the Cuban), Clive Lawson. And not one of these people was ever told exactly what it was that we were putting together in the Caribbean. . . .

The Rose Diary

The saying "Mad dogs and Englishmen" obliquely refers to the fact that our sun will cook you like bacon. Beware!

Sign on Beach at Turtle Bay

April 29, 1975; Coastown, San Dominica

TUESDAY, THE FIRST DAY OF THE SEASON

Not by coincidence, April 29, 1975, marked the end of the most spectacularly newsworthy trial ever held on the eighty-one-by-thirty-nine-mile Caribbean island of San Dominica.

26

Parts of the pyrotechnic high court scene were hard to imagine, or describe.

For a beginning, the plain, tiny courtroom is packed to its high, square beam rafters. The room is noisy as a sporting event, but with slow-turning *Casablanca* fans up on the ceiling for the sharpest possible contrast.

Then there is the matter of the most perversely interesting of the defendants—fifteen-year-old Leon Rachet.

The five-foot, six-inch teen-ager has a slate-black, intelligent face that is at the same time piggy and cruel. He has long black corn-locks, sopping wet all through the trial, dripping at the ends like frayed rope just rained on.

At least once every five minutes the boy's grandmother, his guardian, punctuates the final proceedings with a loud, pitiful scream from her seat in the courtroom gallery. "Leon!" she shouts. "My bway Leon! Oh no, son!"

"You are murdering curs without any shame that I can make out." Seventy-year-old Judge André Dowdy is meanwhile lecturing the teen-ager and the two grown men standing beside him.

"I feel no mercy toward any of you. Not even toward you, boy. I consider you all mad dogs. . . ."

Flanking Rachet on either side, thirty-year-old Franklin Smith aimlessly shifts his weight from one orange work boot to the other; Chicki Holt—father of fourteen children by five women, the local newspapers like to reprint with every new story on the trial—just stares up at the plain white ceiling. The slow fans. Frankly, Chicki is bored.

Eight months earlier, the same three men had stood outside a stammering Volkswagen Superbug one mile from the country town of New Burg.

They'd robbed an American tourist named Francis Cichoski, a fireman from Waltham, Massachusetts, on a golfing vacation.

At the end of the broad-daylight holdup, one of the three blacks had knocked the white man down with the business side of a sugar-cane machete. The blow had killed Cichoski instantly. Then the man's white, crew-cut head had been chopped off and left sitting on its cheek in the blacktop road.

In the eight months since then, the motivation for the New Burg murder had been described as racial unrest; economic unrest; sex unrest; blood lust; obeah; soul music and kinky reggae; insanity; and, finally, as the unsubtle beginning of a terrifying Pan-Caribbean revolution. These were not mutually exclusive, it was understood.

Recently, however, San Dominican Prime Minister Joe Walthey had simplified the sociological aspects of the crime.

"No matter what else," the dictatorial black said over rolling, blipping, island TV, "these three men must hang, or this island shall never find peace with itself again. Mark my words on this.

"The life of Francis Cichoski must be avenged," Walthey repeated three times in a row before he finally faded off the television screen.

At 10:30 A.M., Judge André Dowdy reads his verdict in an unsteady, emotion-packed voice.

"All three of you men—Franklin Smith, Donald 'Chicki' Holt, Leon Elmore Rachet," he reads, "are found guilty of the murder as presented in evidence before me and this court. All of you must go to the Russville jail, and there be hanged no more than one week from today. May God have mercy on your souls. And on my own."

"An' on yo' ahss too!" young Leon Rachet suddenly

screams out in the hushed courtroom. "An' on yo' ahss, Dow'dy mon."

Franklin Smith turns to the teen-ager, winces, and says, "Oohh, Leon, mon."

At 10:40, the dull gray roof of the Potts Rum Factory blows off like a slapstick comedian's hat, then flashes leaping flames of orange and red fire up into the balmy, clear blue sky.

Literally within minutes, the Coastown factory is gone; an entire block of the capital city is hopelessly ablaze.

At eleven on the nose, two white foremen are beaten senseless with ball bats at the Cow Park Bauxite Mines.

A hundred car windows are smashed in an executive parking lot.

The executive dining room is rushed and all the prime ribs and hot Southern-fried chicken is either taken away or destroyed.

Inside the courtroom in Coastown, meanwhile, Franklin Smith and Chicki Holt scream obscenely at Judge Dowdy. Their already hoarse, long-haired American lawyer screams at the elderly judge too.

They call him "mama's man"; "runny ass"; "shit pussy"; "blood clot".

Young Leon Rachet stands by quietly, simply watching.

He reaches inside his back pocket and produces a black beret for his sweaty head. At fifteen, he fancies himself part Huey P. Newton, part Selassie, part Che.

During the mad courtroom screaming, he turns to Franklin Smith and tells the older man to shut his "black nager-boy mout."

Strangely, the thirty-year-old man does as he's told.

Outside the cigar-box courthouse, the reggae singer Bob Marley is being blasted from loudspeakers on top of a rainbow-colored VW van.

Marley and his Wailers also yell out of oversized transistor radios along the crowded palm-tree-lined sidewalks.

Angry black faces scream at the courthouse building as if it were alive. Rude Boys in the crowd carry posters promoting the cause of the revolutionary colonel Monkey Dred, and also His Imperial Majesty Haile Selassie. Pretty, innocent-faced schoolchildren wave beautiful hand-painted banners—GO HOME ADMIRAL NELSEN; GO HOME LAURENCE ROCKEFELLER; SAN DOMINICA A BLACK REPUBLIC.

Shiny-faced city policemen march up Court Street behind see-through riot shields.

People throw ripe fruit at the police. Mangoes, green coconuts, small melons.

A nut-skinned man in army fatigues runs up and makes a bizarre, contorted face into the lens of a TV camera.

"Aaahh deangerous!" he shouts, and becomes famous across the world.

At 11:15, a row of five Hertz Rent-A-Cars is blown up with *plastique* at Robert F. Kennedy Airport outside Coastown.

At 11:30, the three black murderers are led out onto the shiny white courthouse porch.

The San Dominican Terrors are about to begin in earnest.

Fifteen-year-old Leon Rachet has on a Day-Glo flowered shirt and dark Tonton Macoute sunglasses. His black beret is tipped slightly over one eye. *Deangerously.*

At first, Rachet smiles broadly, waving his handcuffs high over his head like a prize-fight winner.

Then, as the police push him down the glaring white steps, the boy begins literally to scream at the sky.

"Dred kill yo', mon! Monkey kill al yo'! Slit al yo' troats." Over and over the boy screams out the name of an island revolutionary.

"Monkey Dred slit me own auntie's throat. Ay-ee! Ay-ee!"

Suddenly, a well-dressed black man in the crowd screams out above all the other noise.

"Gee-zass, mon. Oh, Gee-zass Ky-rist!"

Someone has thrown a sun-catching, silver Frisbee high up into the air. It's curving down into the crowd around the handcuffed murderers.

And as fifteen-year-old Leon Rachet reaches the bottom of the courthouse steps—with the back door of a black police Rover flung open to receive him; with eyes turning up toward the suddenly descending silver Frisbee—a white man in a Panama suit and hat steps out of the crowd and fires three shots into the mad boy's face.

Watching the strange, possessed teen-ager crumple up and fall, standing in a large group of white tourists behind police lines, Carrie Rose can only hope the rest of the Terrors will go so smoothly.

Robert F. Kennedy Airport; Coastown, San Dominica

TUESDAY EVENING

At 9:45 that night, an American Airlines Boeing 727 begins a light, feathery approach down into San Dominica's Robert F. Kennedy Airport.

The massive silver plane glides in amazingly low over the blue-black Caribbean.

Big red lights blink at one-second intervals on the plane's wings and tail. The red lights reflect beautifully off the dark-blue sea.

Hidden in blackness beside a filling station near Runway Number 2, Damian Rose watches the pretty landing with considerable interest. He runs through his final plan one more time.

Meanwhile, out on Runway 1, the tires of the 727 are already touching down with the slightest bump and grind. A half-stoned calypso band begins to play up near the main terminal.

The airplane's wheels screech as its brakes and thrust-reversal system take hold.

And as the plane reaches a point halfway to its landing mark, Damian Rose is forced to make his decision.

Raising an expensive German-made rifle to his

cheek, he gets a small dark box on the runway into the clear greenish light of his night scope.

He fires once, twice, three times.

The unsophisticated bomb on the runway goes off, drowning out the rifle explosions, blowing away a large section of the airplane's belly.

As the 727 rolls to a stop, flames burst from its midsection, then out the windows over its wings.

Doors fly open and emergency escape equipment tumbles outside.

Screaming passengers start to come out of the airplane, some of them on fire.

The airport's two emergency trucks head out toward the burning plane, slowly at first, their inexperienced drivers not believing what they're seeing.

An unidentifiable person's burning head is in one of the plane's tiny windows.

A white woman on fire runs across the dark Tarmac, looking like a burning cross.

A stewardess stands at one door with her fingers buried in her frosted-blond hair, screaming for help.

Four hours later—when the fire is finally out—six people from the 727 are dead, more than fifty others have been burned, and nobody on the island has a clue why it's happened.

The next day the puzzle seems to become a hair clearer.

COUPLE SLAIN ON BEACH

In 1967, when we were selling fifty- and hundred-milligram bags of heroin, Damian told me that he aspired to be the greatest criminal mind in the world. He said that the world was ripe for a criminal hero: brilliant, with a little raffish touch of William H. Bonney—a little Butch Cassidy gilding. . . . I liked that idea very much. I got to be Katharine Ross in the fantasy.

The Rose Diary

April 30, 1975; Turtle Bay, San Dominica

WEDNESDAY AFTERNOON, THE SECOND DAY OF THE SEASON

On the macadam highway that slices through Turtle Bay, Peter Macdonald—a young man who is to play a large part in things to come—makes his daily bicycle ride through lush, sun-streaked paradise.

As he pedals a ten-speed, Lucky Strike-green Peugeot, Macdonald is enjoying the extra luxury of recalling several foolish glories out of his past.

Nearly twenty-five years old, Peter rides well enough, and looks healthy, anyway. Physically, he's an attention-getter.

Pleasantly muscular, six foot one, he rides in holey

gray gym shorts with "Property of U.S.M.A. West Point" printed in gold on one leg.

He wears ragged Converse All-Star sneakers from Herman Spiegel's Sportin' Supplies in Grand Rapids, Michigan. . . .

. . . Gray-and-red snowbird socks that make his feet peel their yellowing calluses.

. . . A bent, dusty Detroit Tigers souvenir hat that looks as if it's been worn every day of his life. And nearly has been.

Underneath the baseball hat, his chestnut-colored hair is cut short, very high up on the sides. It's a real throwback haircut—a cut they used to call a "West Pointer."

Nearly everything about Peter Macdonald is throwback: his young lumberjack's good looks, his High Episcopal morals, philosophies, Midwestern-farmer stubbornness; everything except for the last four months, anyway—the time he's spent on San Dominica —the four months he's been a lackey-bartender, a beachcomber, a fornicator. Quite frankly, a nothing.

As he passes through the island hills, gnats begin to swim in the sweat of his strong back.

Peter the Ridiculous, his girl friend, Jane Cooke, likes to say in private places.

Once upon a time, Peter had run around Michigan like that: *quitely, desperately, ridiculous* . . . in winter . . . in ten-pound, black-rubber sea boots.

Once upon a time he'd been an Army brat—the last of the six Macdonald brothers, the last of the Super Six; then he'd been a West Point cadet; then a Special Forces sergeant in Vietnam and Cambodia.

Old foolish glories.

When the high weeds and banana plants start to get too thick—buggy, disturbingly itchy—Peter rides closer to the sea, on the wrong side of the two-lane Shore Highway.

Getting tired now, he considers. Control breaking down. Rhythm going all to hell. Paradise Lost.

He looks down on the starry Caribbean—Turtle Bay —and thinks that he'll take a swim after his ride. Find Jane, maybe, and take a dip with her . . . maybe talk her into spending the afternoon in bed.

Getting very, very tired now, though. Knees threatening to wipe out his chin. Pedals falling flat as pancakes.

Stik-shhh, stik-shhh, stik-shhh, stik-shhh . . .

Shiny with sweat, Peter comes around a sharp bend in the highway . . . and sees Damian Rose.

Thirty yards ahead of him on the road.

A tall blond man standing with a rifle in the crook of his arm. Looking out over the sea.

Peter's first thought: The blond man is enjoying some impromptu hunting. Pigs, most likely.

Parked a little way up the road he can see the man's car. Green sedan. License plate CY and a few numbers.

Local? . . . Haven't seen him around. . . . Must be renting a villa. . . . Looks rich enough. Snobby, too . . .

For some reason, Peter takes the man to be an Englishman. . . . He sees the flash of a tag marked "Harrods" inside the man's jacket. . . . The Tall Blond Englishman. Smashing.

As he passes by, the blond man turns and yells out to him. Almost as if he'd been in a trance.

He yells, "Constitutional!" Some long word . . .

Macdonald takes it for a greeting. Waves. Keeps riding.

Actually, he even picks up his speed a little. The slightest show-off move: Daniel Morelon imitation . . . *That saved him, they said.*

The whole scene takes less than fifteen seconds.

Fifteen mind-bending, life-changing seconds.

Then, another turn down the Shore Highway—bicycle moving downhill like a bat now, whistling—Peter is startled by a loud thrashing in the Kelly-green bush leading down to the beach.

Expecting a little band of goats, some wild pigs, he sees two sweating, barebacked blacks running up the hill.

One of the men, the Cuban, is covered with blood. Smeared with it like finger paints.

All of which will eventually send tremendous shock waves through the CIA, the Cosa Nostra, the San Dominican government. . . . At a cost of one and a quarter million dollars, the Roses aren't supposed to leave witnesses.

As for Peter Macdonald, he's in trouble . . . but at least he's on the run.

In Paris, he would sleep no more than three or four hours during the months before we left for the Caribbean. Usually, he'd go to bed around five in the mornlng. Until then, he'd just be sitting in front of a bright, gooseneck lamp, turned so it was almost in his face. *Thinking things through.* He'd sleep three or four hours, then be up by nine at the latest. Thinking some more about the machetes.

The Rose Diary

Michael O'Mara and his wife, Faye, are walking very, very slowly.

Sand worshippers, they plod westward, from cove to shining cove.

Sixty-year-old Faye hums absently to herself. She makes up a silly tune for "She sells sea shells by the seashore."

From a distance, Mike and Faye look like two old

men down on the beach . . . as they turn a sharp bend, and enter Turtle Bay.

"No wonder I'm so damn achy and tired," Mike says, hitching his baggy, electric-blue swim trunks every fourth or fifth step, walking with his feet splayed out like a large, arthritic duck.

"I can't sleep at these goddamn, ridiculous hotel prices. Who can sleep at forty . . . no. What is it? Fifty? . . . No—forty. Say *thirty* dollars every time you snooze. . . . I'll wait'll Coastown to sleep at those prices. At those prices, I'll wait'll we get back home if I have to."

"Ha, ha." Faye laughs right into the long ash of Mike's cigar. "That's very humorous, Miguel."

She stoops to pick up a nutmeg sea shell, and her stomach bounces like a beach ball in her one-piece.

"Ha. Ha. Ha. That really cracks me up. Hee, hee. See, I'm laughing."

"Laugh away. Room in Coastown's thirty bucks for a double. Europeen plan. That place I think I could sleep maybe. Shit fire and save matches. Skip eatin' dinners altogether. Cut out the goat steaks easy enough. . . . "

Which part Faye doesn't really hear—not this time around on the familiar broken, skipping record: Mike. Instead, the big, white-haired lady seems annoyed at the shell she's just found.

"I hate some people." She weighs the tiny shell scientifically in her palm. "The way they make ashtrays out of these beautiful things. Nature's wonders. Such a waste. And *sooo* tacky."

Mike O'Mara briefly examines his wife's new treasure. Thinks he hears somebody coming. Looks off toward the bushes. Nothing. Can't see worth a shit any more.

He drops her sea shell in the rope net bag he's

dragging along the hot sand. Beginning to feel a little like a Fairmount Park sanitation man, he thinks. *Asshole sea shells.*

"Who gets this work of art?" he asks in a seldom-used, nonshouting voice—the voice he uses as "Good Old Mike," doorman and purveyor of good will at the Rittenhouse Club in Philadelphia.

"That one goes to Libby Gibbs." Faye stoops for another shell, a rose murex, she thinks. "Uhnn . . . Which leaves Aunt Betsy. Bobo. Yacky. And Mama."

Mike stoops down, splashes cool water around his ankles. Pink, swollen, starting-to-blister ankles. *Damn. Jaysus Christ Almighty. Was he actually paying good money to be tortured like this?*

When he straightens up, though, he takes his wife's soft, flabby upper arm. Dammit, he owes her this trip. He really does. Second honeymoon? Whatever you want to call it.

"Faye Wray," he says. "It's just that I don't understand why we have to fly away to some island. . . . Then buy presents for everybody and their brother . . . Now if this was the Christmas Islands . . ."

Suddenly, Faye O'Mara looks awfully sad and tired. She's thinking that her kids don't care any more. Mike certainly doesn't care. Nobody in this big wide world cares a whit what she thinks about anything.

"Aren't you having fun here, Mike?" she asks, for real. *Serious.* Then the bucktoothed Irishwoman grins —the eternal struggle between the two of them— *sharing that . . . something . . .* making her smile and feel tender toward Mike.

The answer to her question never comes, though.

Because Mike O'Mara is running for the first time in fifteen years. Huffing and puffing forward, looking like his knees are locked, don't bend.

He's disbelieving his eyes. Waving for Faye to stay back. "Go back, Faye. Go back."

The Season of the Machete

Because the Philadelphia doorman has found a bloody machete driven halfway to China in the sand. He's found the two hippies who've been killed and mutilated by the Cuban and Kingfish Toone.

And so has a hungry band of wild goats.

We forget that policemen are relatively simple-minded human beings for the most part. Damian says that they are basically unequipped to deal with the creative personality (criminal). It's impossible for them now, and it's getting worse. An amoral generation is coming up fast. Can another police state be far behind?

The Rose Diary

WEDNESDAY EVENING

It's getting dark fast, *black-and-blue-and-pink out over the Caribbean,* when the chief of San Dominica's police force comes to see about the extraordinary machete murders.

Twenty or so less important policemen and Army officials have already arrived. They're deployed all over the beach like survey engineers.

Taking notes. Making measurements. Spreading out litters and yellow rubber sheets that look like rain slickers from a distance.

The policemen's white pith helmets float through the crowd like Carnival balloons.

Before he does anything else, the chief of police stops and counts the valuable helmets on the heads of his men.

Then Dr. Meral Johnson quietly pushes himself through a buzzing ring of bathing suits and cut-off blue jeans; bald heads and brown freckled décolletage; double-knit leisure suits and pantsuits and flowing Empire dresses.

At least four hundred very frightened, very confused vacationers have gathered on the finger-cove beach.

To get a look at the bodies.

And then not to believe their own eyes; not to believe their luck.

Once he's inside the circus of people, Dr. Johnson stops to catch his breath.

He lights up a stumpy black Albertson pipe. *Pup, pup, pup, pup . . .*

The Americans are restless tonight! He makes a small joke, then quickly feels very bad about it. Very bad. Awful.

A little less than five foot ten, four-eyed, seersuckered, 250 pounds, Meral Johnson looks rather tenuous as a policeman, he knows. Tenuous, or is it timorous?

More like a proper, stern, West Indian schoolmaster —which he's been—than a Joseph Wambaugh–style policeman come to solve grisly murders. More like a hick Islander who polishes his shoes with palm oil, his teeth with baking soda.

Well, so be it, Meral Johnson thinks to himself. So be it.

The massive policeman thereupon enters the machete Terrors.

Almost instantly, the flustered German manager of the nearby Plantation Inn begins to shout at him.

"What takes you so long? Now you stop to smoke a pipe."

Dr. Johnson pays the hotel manager as much attention as some sandfly buzzing around his trouser cuffs.

Speaking to none of his subordinates first, the police

chief begins to walk around the yellow rubber sheets that cover bits and pieces of the teen-agers' bodies.

After his short walk, the police chief stands with his back to the sea, simply *watching* the scene of the double murder. Trying to bring his mind back down to an even keel.

The manager of the Plantation Inn has apparently ordered his waiters to cordon off the bodies of the two young people.

The waiters, mostly old blacks with fuzzy white crew cuts—earning less than $30 a week in salary— stand at parade-ground attention in their stiff white dinner jackets.

Each man has on black dress shoes with especially shiny toes. Each holds a flaming torch removed from the inn's dining veranda.

Each of the waiters looks sad and dignified, and above all respectful of the terrible occasion.

The scene is extraordinary—both colonial and primitive—and Johnson wants to be certain he has it reproduced, *burned into his optic nerve,* before he begins the thumb-screwing work ahead of him this night.

What a sight—tragedy, mystery. The worst he's ever come upon.

First, Dr. Johnson approaches the inexperienced, very frightened constable of Turtle Bay District.

Almost since he has arrived, twenty-eight-year-old Bobbie Valentine has been kneeling among the rubber sheets, looking like a mourner, looking as if he might be sick to his stomach.

Now Meral Johnson kneels and speaks to the man in a clear, relatively clean, Oxbridge accent. No trace of island patois.

"What is your thought here, Bobbie?" he asks. A short pause, then he answers his own question. "I think Colonel Dred, perhaps. He's contacted the newspapers and claimed responsibility, at least."

Before the constable has a chance to agree or disagree, the German hotel manager is speaking over both of their heads.

"*I am* Maximilian Westerhuis," he announces with authority—almost titular emphasis. "I manage this nearby Plantation Inn. These two dead . . ."

The large black policeman stands up faster than seems possible. His dark eyes flash. Looking convincingly nasty, Johnson says the first thing that enters his head.

"You wish to make a confession here?"

Westerhuis takes a confused step backwards. "Of course not . . . confessions . . . Don't be absurd with me. . . ."

"Then I am talking to this very good policeman now." Dr. Johnson's voice returns to its usual polite whisper. "Please wait for me, Mr. Westerhuis. On the far side of your service crew."

The inn manager, tall, white-blond, says nothing further. He stalks off angrily.

"Nazi," Johnson mutters—an obvious idea that nonetheless goes completely over the head of Constable Valentine.

"I must do something about this crowd," Johnson then mutters. "Something smart would be preferable."

Smoking his black pipe, the police chief starts to walk from sheet to sheet again.

Very gently, he lifts the bulky rubber covers, then puts them back exactly as they've been. It looks almost as if the policeman is checking on small, sleeping children.

He stays over the severed head of the young woman for what seems like an awfully long time.

Shining a small pocket light, he examines the bloody

face and skull. He uses his fingers first. Then something that appears to be a nail file, but is actually the tamper for his pipe.

The crowd of hotel guests becomes silent as he works.

Every man and woman watches him, but the police chief never looks up at them. For the first time in hours, you can hear birds in the air at Turtle Bay; you can hear the sea lapping.

Finally, with his head still down, respectful as the old black waiters, Dr. Johnson walks back to his constable.

He's spent the previous ten minutes, the entire slow dance back through the mutilated bodies, simply trying to gain some confidence from this crowd. To give them the impression that he's handled murders like this one before.

Now, maybe, he can begin some kind of investigation, at least.

He starts by wriggling the sugar-cane machete out of the sand. He holds the sharp broadsword up to the light of the moon.

"Hmmm," he mutters out loud. "Make sure no one takes any souvenirs." He speaks in a lower voice to Constable Bobbie Valentine. "Americans like souvenirs of disasters. We learned at least that much at the airplane fire. . . .

"And one final thing, Bobbie. Will you spread this word for me? . . . If any of these men sell their hats for souvenirs, tell them they'll be selling pukka beads and sea shells on the streets by this time tomorrow night. I counted sixteen hats coming down here!"

Coastown, San Dominica

At 7:45, the young man who looks like Montgomery Clift sits alone at a shadowy table on the veranda of the Coastown Princess Hotel.

Sipping a Cutty Sark and Perrier water, tapping his swizzle stick to the soft calypso beat of "Marianne," Brooks Campbell is starting to get nervous.

Small problem: he's afraid the other people on the patio are beginning to notice him sitting there all by his lonesome.

Slightly larger problem: his Afro-haired waiter is hassling him, trying to get him to leave so a bigger party can sit at the table.

Very large problem: Damian Rose is half an hour late for their first, presumably their only, face-to-face meeting.

Brooks Campbell doesn't know all the details about Turtle Bay yet, but the general way the Roses are working is beginning to grate on him. At first, there were only supposed to be ten or twelve deaths on San Dominica. Something like the 1973 uprisings on St. Croix . . . Now it looks as it will be worse than that. Much worse. Rose is handling everything his own, idiosyncratic way, and that's why Campbell has asked for the meeting. Demanded a meeting.

At 8:15, Damian Rose still hasn't appeared.

Campbell sits and watches a huge artificial waterfall dump endless gallons of water into an epic swimming pool directly below the patio. He watches couples in bathing suits wind their way along pretty paths lined with palm and casuarina trees.

The small combo is playing a reggae tune now—"The Harder They Come." Revolutionary music.

By 8:45, Brooks Campbell realizes that he isn't going to meet Damian Rose.

Campbell has a sneaking suspicion that no one is ever going to see the mysterious soldier of fortune.

At nine o'clock, the handsome thirty-one-year-old pays his bar bill at the Princess.

He walks the twelve blocks to the U.S. Embassy; hears war drums in the air out on the streets. Back at the Embassy, he's greeted with the most disturbing news of his career.

Someone has seen a tall blond man at Turtle Bay that afternoon.

Someone has finally seen the face of Damian Rose.

Turtle Bay, San Dominica

The field machete left in the sand at Turtle Bay is half scythe, half butcher's cleaver.

From the look of it, it's seen heavy use on a sugar plantation or in the West Hills jungle. The knife part is twenty-six inches long, four inches wide. Heavy-duty steel. The wooden handle is seven inches, warped, badly nickered, with big rivets like a kitchen carving knife. When it's held in one hand, the machete brings to mind cutlasses and sword-fighting.

Sitting in the paperback library at the Plantation Inn, Dr. Meral Johnson examines the sharp knife for a long time.

He tolds it close up to a bright reading lamp. He whips it through the air, cutting at shadows. *Scary weapon*. Johnson has personally seen a machete cut a goat in half at a swipe.

The weary policeman plops down in an old Morris chair in the library. He begins to sort through some of the loose, contradictory details of the case . . . the Turtle Bay massacre. The American Airlines bombing. The curious shooting of Leon Rachet.

Right then, the best Dr. Johnson figures he can do

is concentrate on details that might lead him or the Army to the island revolutionary, Monkey Dred. He instructs his men to do the same in their investigations.

It's an honest but costly mistake—and one the Roses have counted on.

. . . *Policemen are relatively simple-minded human beings.* . . .

Witnesses.

A tennis pro and his wife from Saddle River, New Jersey, had seen a black hobo on the beach near the time of the machete murders.

An elderly Englishwoman saw a group of "unruly native boys" congregating in the royal palms just beyond the inn's main stretch of beach.

A couple from Georgia remember seeing an old black man with some mangy goats on a rope leash.

A pretty eleven-year-old girl is brought to Dr. Johnson because she has a story, her mother says. The girl explains that around eight o'clock that evening, she'd locked herself in her mother's suite. Then, she'd screamed bloody murder until one of the hotel bartenders—Peter Macdonald—came and broke down the door with a fire ax. The girl's mother, an actress, wants the police chief to get both of them on an airplane back to New York that evening. Crying, occasionally screaming at the black man, she says that her daughter is about to have a nervous breakdown.

Simultaneously, another group of "witnesses" is being questioned inside the inn's main business office.

"You're one of the bartenders here." Constable Bobbie Valentine speaks softly at first. The country policeman is sitting behind a Royal office typewriter, only occasionally glancing up from his note pad. "Talk to me, mon."

In as few words as possible, Peter Macdonald tries

to explain what he's seen bike-riding up on the Shore Highway that afternoon.

He describes Damian Rose as English-looking: a *Tall Blond Englishman.*

He tells the constable about the two blacks who'd come up from the beach dripping blood. He mentions the expensive German rifle; the green sedan; he even describes the coat from Harrods in London.

When he's finished, the black constable seems to be smirking. Looking at Peter as if he's just another American nut on the loose. A crank case.

"Dat's good, mon," the policeman says. "Next, please," he calls out the open office door.

Peter can feel himself starting to get a little angry.

"Hey, could you wait a minute?" he says. "Slow down for just a second, please. Okay? I understand that you're seeing a lot of very upset people tonight. I know it's crazy around here. . . . But what about this Englishman?"

"I took notes." The black man holds up his pad. "Anyway, we already know about dem killers. Colonel Dred. Badass. You know about Dred, mon? Nah, you don't know 'bout Dred."

"I don't know much about him." Peter tries to break through to the policeman. "But I saw a blond *white* man up there where they killed those two poor kids. I saw a lot of blood on a couple of black guys who looked like they'd just strangled a grammar-school class with their bare hands. I got scared, and I don't get scared very easily."

Once again the policeman seems to be smirking. He's so know-it-all in his attitude Peter just wants to rap him.

"I know, mon. I know it. Blond Englishmon type. Tall. Green car license starts CY. Check it out for you, mon. Check it out . . . okay—*who's next with stories here?*"

And as the only legitimate witness walks out of the investigation . . . as the unbelievable confusion and mistakes just start to mount . . . Dr. Meral Johnson wanders out on the dark Plantation Inn grounds.

Headhunter hunter, pith-helmet counter, basically a good man, the police chief is convinced that the bloody revolution has finally come to Calypsoland. He tries to put his mind in the head of the criminal, but he can honestly find no points of commonality. Quite obviously he's dealing with a psychotic madman in Dred.

Even the tree frogs seem to be crazy on this night.

People never want to die, for some strange reason. Especially young people. Especially young, unfulfilled singles on vacations they can't afford . . . Originally, we'd planned the first machete murders for the island's version of Club Méditerranée. The Plantation Inn was chosen because of secondary considerations.

The Rose Diary

Turtle Bay, San Dominica

In the noisy background of the Plantation Inn's Cricket Lounge, a young, bone-tanned woman complains that she'll never be able to shut her eyes and catch some rays at a beach again.

"Two murders. Just like the movies," someone is saying—a short-haired man with a coke spoon dangling around his neck.

Up at the lounge bar, Peter Macdonald talks to his girl friend, Jane Cooke. He also serves up gallons of Planter's and Boom Boom Punch; rum toddies; Jamaica coffee; swizzles; Fog-Cutters—plus an amazing quantity of good old-fashioned neat whisky.

"I know how paranoid this sounds," he says to Jane, "but the police didn't seem to want to listen."

"That constable took your statement. He did, didn't he?"

"Yeah. I guess. But he seemed to have the whole thing wrapped up, Janie. Colonel Dred. Colonel Dred. Forget everything else. The tall blond man. The fancy rifle. Jesus, I don't know. I *hope* they're right. . . . It's just that they weren't very professional about it. It was like 'Ted Mack's Amateur Hour' in there."

"Ahhh Pee-ter, mon."

The lilting voice of the lounge calypso singer drifts across the room.

Then the singer whistles into his microphone. He taps the mike with a long, effeminate fingernail. Blows softly into strange, snakey, bamboo pipes.

"No need be afraid of Leon," he whispers to his white audience. Couples out of John O'Hara and John Marquand. Lots of bright Waspy green in their outfits—green and Bermuda pink.

He sings to them. "San Dominic' woman's love day say . . . is lak a mornin' dew. . . . Jus' as lakly it fall on de horse's turd . . . as on de rose."

The singer laughs. A pretty fair imitation of Geoffrey Holder.

A few people in the dark, red-lanterned bar start to clap.

Peter Macdonald pulls at a bicycle bell hidden somewhere in the liquor bottles over the bar.

"I wan' to sing yo' peoples lubbley song 'bout sech a ooman," the singer goes on. " 'Bout her rose. An' . . . well, yo know it, my friends . . . de unworty objet ub dat gal's affection. Me own rival. *A real shit!*"

At the same time, Chief of Police Meral Johnson walks down damp stone stairs, then along a row of cells in the dimly lit medieval basement of the Coastown jail.

Walking behind him is a line-up of seven policemen and clerks. Nearly everyone in the Coastown jail at that late hour.

The somber parade turns down another row of cells. Then another. At the end of the third row, a tall, perspiring constable waits beside an open, steel-plated door.

Inside the cell, the chief of police can already see the white man who'd shot Leon Rachet the previous morning.

The mysterious, middle-aged white man is lying on his cot with both arms spread wide. His hairy bare legs dangle off one end of the bed. A puddle of urine and blood runs out of the cell, right down a big drain in the dirty corridor.

While Dr. Johnson has been out at the Plantation Inn, the man has been murdered.

Killed in his bed. In jail. By a sugar-cane machete.

The crude knife is sticking out of the dead man's hairy belly—a red wool cap carefully hung on its hilt.

"Monkey Dred," Johnson whispers.

"Pee-ter! Pee-ter!"

The calypso singer's sweet voice drifts across the Cricket Lounge.

"Tell me dis one ting, mon? . . . What be de difference be-tween Irishmon wedding, an' Irishmon wake?"

Sulking, a little embarrassed, Peter resists.

He doesn't want to be a part of the show tonight. Not tonight. Not with the image of the mutilated nineteen-year-olds crawling through his mind like blood worms.

"So what's the difference?" someone calls out from the dark bar.

Peter looks at Jane and can see the same—what? Distaste? Nausea?

"One less drunk!" The chestnut-haired man finally gives in; yanks the asinine bicycle bell, feels—very strangely, dumbly—a little homesick.

TOURISTS FLEE RESORT HOTELS!

"Go from Slush to Lush!"
Magazine Ad for
San Dominica

Nine murders were reported around the resort island on the third day.

Two knifings; two pistol shootings; a forced drowning; four machete killings.

Sophisticated TV news crews began to arrive on San Dominica in the early afternoon: hippie cameramen, soundmen who looked like NASA engineers, "California Dreaming" directors, assistant directors, reporters, and commentators. Crews came from ABC, CBS, NBC. They came from local stations in New York City, Miami, and Chicago. Apparently, the machete murders were an especially popular item in Chicago and New York.

Reporters and crew members were given hazardous-duty pay just like they received for combat assignments, urban riots, or for covering madmen on the loose.

Newspaper correspondents—quieter types, less Los Angelese—started to arrive too.

They came from the States, of course, but they also began to come in from Western Europe; from Africa and Asia; and especially from South America. The Third World countries were particularly well represented.

The newshounds smelled a revolution!

Meanwhile, police and Army experts were predicting that the sudden, mind-boggling violence would either die down completely—or flare up all over the Caribbean.

So far—even with Colonel Dred as an obvious target —it was a hell of a mystery.

We had learned long before we ever saw the Caribbean that beautiful scenery provides the most chilling background for any kind of terrorism.

The Rose Diary

May 1, 1975; Titchfield Cove, San Dominica

THURSDAY MORNING, THE THIRD DAY OF THE SEASON

Dressed in loose-fitting blue jeans and a blue-cotton T-shirt, Damian Rose climbs hard, and as fast as possible. He moves toward huge outcroppings of black rock poised above the Shore Highway.

At Titchfield Cove, this time. Not half a mile from the island's chic Club Méditerranée.

High up in the rocks, the lazy island trade winds have chiseled two primitive heads over centuries and centuries—neither of which, Rose is thinking as he moves along, has been worth the hot air and bother.

His fingers curled into small cracks, Rose pulls himself up over countless tiny ledges toward the sea-blue sky. He can feel his boots crunching loose rocks as he goes; he can taste his own salty sweat.

After fifteen minutes of hard climbing, he pulls himself onto a barren ledge of flat rock. The small jut of rock is about four feet long, less than three feet wide. Close up, the black rock is loaded with specks of shiny mica. Mica, and tiny sea-gull bones.

From the high gull's burial ground, Damian can see everything he needs to see.

The morning after the Turtle Bay murders has turned out crisp and pure, with a high blue sky all over the Caribbean. A hawk flies directly over his head, watching the empty highway, it seems, watching him.

Way down below, the sea is choppy in spite of the pacific blue skies. Brown reefs are visible on the outskirts of Titchfield Cove.

There's a long, dramatic stretch of crystal beach that ends in another hill of high black rocks.

Damian Rose begins to concentrate on a slightly balding dark-haired man and his two children walking down on the perfect beach.

The three of them are getting their feet and legs wet in the creamy surf . . . walking along as if they're waiting for the man who photographs such moments for post and greeting cards.

Damian takes out two lengths of streamlined black pipe.

He begins to screw them together. Makes a barrel. Screws the longer pipe into a lightweight stock. Makes a gun. Adds a sniper's scope from his backpack.

The dark-haired man, Walter Marks, dives over a small blue wave and disappears.

His boy and little girl seem leery of the water. Attractive children, Rose bothers to notice. Two blonds, like their mother.

Their father is an ass to take them out the morning after the machete killings. A shallow, foolish ass. Promised them a vacation. Always keeps his promises.

Rose puts the sight of the German rifle to his eye. Thin crosshairs that don't meet.

He watches Marks's slick brown hair surface in bubbles.

The man stands up and the water is only to his waist. He has a very hairy chest: brown hair that seems to turn black in wet tufts.

Through the powerful Zeiss sight, Walter Marks seems close enough to reach out and touch.

Rose sees the Cuban waving from high weeds not far behind the beach.

Shooting goldfish in a bowl: he remembers a strange, wonderful saying.

Damian squeezes off just one shot.

Walter Marks trips over backwards in the three-foot-high water. He looks as if he's trying to step back over a wave to amuse his children.

The bullet has gone through the center of his head, spitting out brain like a corkscrew.

The blond boy and little girl begin to scream at once. The small children hug one another. They seem to be dancing in the suddenly pinkish water.

Then Kingfish and the Cuban appear with the machete. The Roses' inspired buck-and-wing team. Wading out into the sea.

Fortunately, and at the same time unfortunately for the Marks children, there have to be witnesses this time. The witnesses are to be the children themselves.

Too bad, Rose thinks for a split second. And yet perfect.

The Season of the Machete

The cold-blooded murder of the president of ASTA. The public execution of the president of the American Society of Travel Agents.

Who deserves it for being such a pompous fool. For ignoring all the warnings.

Turtle Bay, San Dominica

Somewhere in the U.S. Marine annals, it says that "a Marine on Embassy Duty is an Ambassador in uniform."

Clearly out of uniform—dressed in gray insignia shorts and nothing else—twenty-four Embassy Duty Marines spend the morning of May 1 conducting a dreaded sector search of the beach at Turtle Bay.

The muscular soldiers pick up driftwood, seahorses, periwinkle, clear, rubbery jellyfish. They pick up chewing gun, matches, lint, stomach-turning shreds of human flesh, strands of hair, the nub of a woman's finger. They pick up everything on the beach that isn't sand: literally everything.

They put whatever they find into heavy-duty plastic bags maked XYXYXY.

Then the Marine captain orders his men to "rake the sand back to normal."

Hand-in-hand up on the Shore Highway, Peter Macdonald and Jane Cooke watch the dubious detective work going on all over the beach.

Beside a big man like Macdonald, Jane seems

slighter than she really is. Close up, she's somewhat big-boned—an old-fashioned Midwestern beauty right out of Nelson Algren. Freckles, dimples, long blond hair cut in a river of curls.

Before she'd become a social director at the Plantation Inn, Jane had been a high-school English teacher in Pierre, South Dakota. She'd married another English teacher at twenty-one; miscarried their future Joyce Carol Oates in a Pierre shopping mall; been separated at twenty-three.

After that, Jane had decided to see a little bit more of the world than the Dakota Badlands. She'd traveled down to South America. Traveled up to the Caribbean. Haiti, then San Dominica. Then Peter Macdonald. Crazy, funny Peter—who reminded her of a poem, also a Simon & Garfunkel song, called "Richard Cory."

Before he'd come to the Plantation Inn, Peter had been, first and foremost, the last and least worthy (in his own head, anyway) of six Macdonald brothers. Three college baseball stars, two academic big deals— and then Peter. Little Mac.

As a result, Peter had become a cadet at the U.S. Military Academy at West Point (like his father— Big Mac). He'd left West Point after his Second Class year—become a soldier for real. A Special Forces sergeant; decorated twice; shot in the back once. A war hero—whatever that was in the mid-1970s.

With a little luck and good planning that winter, he'd wound up in the sunny Caribbean. *R&R . . . "Getting your shit together,"* his suddenly contemporary-as-hell father had said in a long letter. . . . He'd met Jane in September and they'd moved in together by the end of the month. Both of them living and working at the ritzy Plantation Inn . . . *Not bad.*

Jane has only one question about the Marines working down on Turtle Bay.

"What in heck do they do it for?"

Peter finds himself smiling.

"Rake dirt? . . . I don't know what for. *They* don't know. *Somebody* probably knew why at one time or another. Now they just do it. Soldiers rake dirt on every military base in the world."

"Well, it's the dumbest thing I've ever seen. One of the dumbest. It's dumber than baseball." Jane grins.

"It's a whole lot dumber when you're behind the rake. That's okay, though. . . . Let's walk. . . . By the way, baseball isn't dumb."

They walk up through a lot of banana and breadfruit trees. Pretty jungle with a few parrots and cockatoos to spice things up. Kling-kling birds, too.

Macdonald takes his baseball cap out of a back pocket and tugs it on to keep out bugs.

"What are you going to do now, Peter?" she finally asks him.

Macdonald sighs. "I don't know what I should do. . . . Maybe the murders were just what the police say. Dassie Dred making sure his people get fair trials from now on. No more hanging sentences. Simple as that."

"And the Englishman?"

"Ah, the bloody white man. The damn, tall, blond, Day-of-the-fucking-Jackal character. Complicating our beautifully uncomplicated existence."

Peter picks up a rock and sidearms a high inside curve around a banana tree.

"You know what else? . . . I'm starting to feel bad about wasting my life all of a sudden. . . . Anything but that, dear God. Please don't make me feel guilty about feeling good. See, I was just in this fucked-up war and . . ."

Jane puts her arms around Peter's slim waist. Behind him she can see sharp blue sea through palm leaves. It's all so perfect that most of the time she doesn't completely believe in it.

"Tell me this, Peter Macdonald. Where does it say that *not killing yourself working* is wasting your life?"

Macdonald smiles at the wise blonde girl. He holds onto one of her soft breasts and kisses her mouth gently.

"I'm not sure. . . . But it's engraved on my brain. I feel that exact thought grinding away in there every day that I'm down here. Every time I dive into the deep blue sea."

He puts his hand over his mouth. When he does that, his voice comes out deep and strange.

"Get yourself a decent job, Macdonald, you bum. Shape up before it's all over, Pete. Be somebody or be gone. . . . Anyway"—his voice goes back to normal—"I guess I have to do something about the Englishman, huh, Laurel?"

Jane winces slightly. In their little South Seas fantasy world—their paradise life in the Caribbean—she's called Laurel; Peter is Hardy-ha-ha.

"I wish you wouldn't," the blonde woman says. "Really. I'm serious, Peter."

"I have to try one more thing anyway," Peter says.

For the moment, though—8:30, Thursday morning—the two of them make a little clearing on the pretty hillside. They lie down together like two missionary lovers.

Peter pulls gently at the white shirt knotted under her breasts. Jane lifts her slender arms. Lets the loose white shirt go up around her neck, shoulders. "I love you so much," she whispers. "Just thought I'd say that."

He takes a soft, cool breast in each hand. Unzips her shorts. Slides shorts and panties down over her dark brown legs.

She unbuckles red L. L. Bean suspenders, pulls at blue jeans, helps him out of underwear and baseball hat. He's kissing her everywhere, tonguing her nipples for a long, lazy time. Feeling soft, invisible down on her stomach. Smelling coconut oil.

Peter enters Jane slowly too, an inch at a time, then long, slow thrusts. . . . They stop each other twice. Delaying, saving. Then they come with little spasms that make them dizzy. A long climax, both of them whispering as if they're in a church.

When they finally sit up again, all the Marines are gone. Turtle Bay looks perfect and innocent again. Raked neat as a farmer's field.

Chuk, chuk, chuk is the sound machetes make cutting sugar cane.

Chik, chik, chik is the sound Peter hears.

Chik, chik, chik.

Chik, chik, chik.

Chik, chik, chik. Cashoo.

Peter has found Maximilian Westerhuis tabulating fancy yellow-on-white hotel bills in his eight-by-eight office, wearing steel-rimmed spectacles, looking somewhat mathematical. A cipher.

The coal-black machine the German uses for counting looks as if it's somehow survived the Weimar Republic. In addition to the machine, there are red-and-blue-edged letter-envelopes scattered all over the inn manager's desk: news from the Fatherland.

Resting on some of the papers is a big foamy mug of Würzburger dark.

Standing in the doorway, Peter is reluctant to announce himself to the huffy young German. Then the pecking on the adding machine stops, and he doesn't have to.

"Peter, what do you want? Can't you see I'm too

busy with all of these fools checking out of the hotel?"

Looking slightly dizzy, the white-blond man eyes him with distaste over the wire rims of his spectacles.

"Macdonald, *what is it you want?*" The strident voice comes once again.

I want to beam myself right back out of your office, Peter is thinking. You're so full of yourself, hot shit and vinegar, that it turns my stomach.

"I have to ask a personal favor," Peter says softly, wincing inside at the toady way the words come out. Playing Heinrich Himmler to Max's Hitler. "I need to borrow your BMW."

The inn manager huffs out a small nose laugh.

"Borrow my motorcycle? Have you gone mad? Leave me alone. Get out of here."

"Yeah, well, in a minute . . . You see, I've got to talk to somebody else about the man I saw on the Shore Highway yesterday. It's bothering me, Max. I've got to find out why in hell they—"

"You talked *to me*, Macdonald," Westerhuis cuts in. "*I* talked to the stupid newspapers people. *You* talked to the policeman last night. People know about your man up on the hill, *nicht wahr?* Now I tell you, *leave*. You don't ever call me Max, by the way."

Peter suddenly cuts off all pretense of diplomacy.

"I want to talk to the American ambassador in Coastown! . . . Lives could be at issue here, Westerhuis. I need your fucking BMW for two or three hours. That's it, you know. Be a human being, huh? Pretend."

The inn manager begins to use one side of his metal office desk like a bass drum.

"Absolutely not!" he pounds. "I thought it over for five seconds, and the answer is *no!* Now get out of here. One more word and I fire you as bartender Johnny on the spot."

Peter turns away and starts out of the claustrophobic office.

"Peter on the spot," he mumbles. "Screw you, you Nazi love-child."

"What is that I hear?" Westerhuis calls out the door after him.

But, then, *chik, chik, chik,* he's operating the antique tabulator again, thinking: *Poor damn fool Peter Macdonald. Poor fool bartender. Should have stayed in the Army for your entire life.*

While outside, an expensive-looking silver key is turning in the ignition of the shiny black BMW motorcycle—Peter Macdonald and Jane Cooke having taken big steps in the wrong crazy direction. Both of them about to jump in way over their heads.

Peter saying, "Sure, Max said it was okay. . . . Hang on tight, here we go!"

Which is, perhaps, the understatement of the decade.

I believe that Damian could be happy in Europe on $10 a day. I could be content, I think, on Jacqueline Onassis' $10,000 a week. Sometimes I find myself reading *Cosmopolitan* and identifying with Jackie. Weird fantasy life! I've even plotted out how I could get to marry one (or more) of the world's richest men. . . . Damian could be wealthy if he cared primarily about money. Damian could be an international film star like Bronson or Clint Eastwood. Or the still-life president of General Motors. Damian could be, Damian could be . . . Sitting on rocks in Crete. Starting to repeat myself as I approach thirty. Scary thoughts for your basic hick out of Nebraska.

The Rose Diary

Coastown, San Dominica

In the middle of a world of hackarounds—fruit and straw vendors, fruits, package-rate tourists, cab-drivers by the gross, beeping double-decker buses— Carrie Rose looks around Politician Square and tries to single out one poor bugger who has to be sacrificed that morning.

She concentrates on ten or so long-haired dopers grazing near the entrance to Wahoo Public Beach.

Here is pure white trash floated down from the United States. . . . Semiacceptable bums in tie-dye REGGAE T-shirts. In LOVE RASTAFARI T-shirts. Drinking out of Blue Label beer cans. Chewing gum to a man. Eating fresh coconut.

Beyond choosing the comatose group, it's all disturbingly arbitrary, Carrie can't help thinking. Depressing. Damian's sort of game.

Finally, she settles on a short, skinny one. A freak's freak among the idle young Americans. Carrie names him the Loner.

The Loner appears to be nineteen or twenty. Dirty jeans and a buckskin vest over his bare, sunken chest. Long, stringy blond hair. Wide moon eyes.

The Loner is also smoking *ganja* right out on the square. Smoking the strong island marijuana like a morning's first cup of Maxwell House.

Carrie Rose stops a schoolboy walking on her side of the triangular street section. A pretty brown boy of eight or nine. Books all neat and nice, held together in a red rubber sling.

She asks him if he has time to earn fifty cents before his classes start that morning.

When the boy says that he does, the beautiful white woman points through the crowds. She directs his eyes until he sees the long-haired white man in the gold vest.

The Loner has moved up against the wall of a paint-scabbing boathouse. *Holding up the walls,* they used to say back in her hometown, Lincoln, Nebraska.

"All you have to do," she explains to the schoolboy, "is take this letter to that man. Give him this five dollars here. Tell him he has to deliver my letter to 50 Bath Street; *50 Bath Street.* . . .

"Now tell me what you have to do for your fifty cents."

The little black boy is very serious and bright. He repeats her instructions exactly. Then the boy's face lights up.

"Hey, missus, I could deliver yo' letter myself."

Carrie's hand sinks deep into her wallet for the money.

"No, no." She shakes her head. "That man over there will do it. And you should tell him that a big black man is watching him. Tell him the letter is going to the black man's girl friend."

"All right. All right. Give me everything. I take it to him all right."

The boy disappears while crossing the square in the hectic, colorful crowd. Carrie panics. Starts to cross the street herself.

Then the boy suddenly resurfaces near the lounging hippies. He approaches the Loner grinning a mile, waving the long yellow envelope.

The long-haired man and the boy negotiate in front of the boathouse.

A buttery sun is rising up just over the building's buckling tin roof. SAN DOMINICA—BEST PLACE IN THE WORLD is painted in red on the shack.

Finally, the Loner accepts the letter.

Carrie sits down on a bench and takes out the morning *Gleaner*. COUPLE SLAIN ON BEACH. Cross-legged, wearing her large horn-rimmed glasses, she's among twenty or thirty tourists reading books and newspapers down a long line of sagging white benches.

The Loner is looking up and down the crowded street for his benefactor. Very paranoid, apparently. Then the man does an odd little bebop step for whoever is watching. "Dyno-mite," they'll find out his nickname later that day.

Finally, the Loner heads off in the direction of Trenchtown District.

To deliver a soon-to-be-famous letter at 50 Bath Street.

The American Embassy in Coastown is wonderfully quiet, Macdonald is thinking.

A little like West Point's Thayer Hall in the lull of summertime. Like the University of Michigan at Ann Arbor, where he'd spent one lonely, lazy summer after the Army.

Green-uniformed security men walk up and down long corridors on the balls of their spongy cordovans. Whispery receptionists whisper to messengers about the latest machete murder. Friendly casuarina trees wave at everybody through rows of bay windows in the library.

Peter passes the plush wood and dark leather furniture in every room and hallway. Heavy brass ashtrays and cuspidors left over from the Teddy Roosevelt era. The smell of furniture polish is everywhere. Lemon Pledge furniture polish and fresh-cut hibiscus and oleander.

Peter decides that it's all very official and impressive —very American, in some ways—but also very cold and funereal.

And frightening.

Dressed in a neatly pressed Harry Truman sports shirt—wind-blown palm trees and sailboats on a powder-blue background—with a permanent flush in his cheeks, Peter is led up to his hearing by a starchy butler type. A haughty black in a blue Holy Communion suit.

Up thick-carpeted stairways. Down deserted passageways with nicely done oil portraits of recent Presidents on all the wall space. Up a winding, creaking, wooden stairway.

Finally, into the doorway of a cozy third-floor office. A neat room where some teen-ager could have had the bedroom of his dreams.

A young man, a public safety adviser, is sitting at a trendy, refinished desk inside the attic room.

Very sun-tanned and handsome, the man strikes Peter as a case study favoring the pseudoscience of reincarnation. *The subconsul is an exact look-alike for the dead American actor Montgomery Clift.*

"Mr. Campbell." The snippy black literally clicks his heels. "A Mr. Peter Macdonald to see you, sir."

"Hi," Peter says.

"I'm sorry to bother you like this."

"No bother. Sit down. Have a seat."

Peter sits on a wine-red settee across from Campbell. Then, talking with a soft Midwestern accent—vaguely aware of the Helter-Skelter horrors and dangers he's officially associating himself with—he begins to tell Brooks Campbell what he's seen.

The two black men chugging up through high brush from the beach at Turtle Bay.

The blood so bright, stop-sign red, it looked as if it had to be paint.

The striking blond man forever framed among sea grapes and royal palms in his mind.

The expensive German-made rifle. The green sedan. The jacket from London . . . All of it happening roughly parallel with the place where the two nineteen-year-olds had been killed and mutilated; had their corpses desecrated beyond belief.

And by the end of the strange, appalling story—new, wonderful sensation!—Peter feels that he's actually been listened to.

This man Campbell is leaning way back in his swivel chair, smoking a True Blue cigarette down to the filter, looking very serious and interested. Looking like a young, troubled senator in his starchy blue shirt with the rolled-up sleeves.

"You said you'd gone around another bend in the Shore Highway." Campbell has a deep, orator's voice. A hint of wealth in it; a slight lockjaw tendency. "Did you see the black men actually join up with this other man? The blond man?"

That was a good point, Peter considers. Not a bad start. He *never had seen* the men actually get together.

"No. I was really going on the bike by then. It wasn't the kind of thing you wanted to stop and . . . Well, you know. . . . The whole thing lasted about thirty seconds."

Peter begins to smile. An involuntary, nervous smile. A serious moment of doubt and vulnerability. He catches himself twisting his sports shirt between his thumb and forefinger.

Campbell sits forward in his swivel chair. He crushes out his cigarette.

"I've got to ask you to take my word about something, Peter." He levels Macdonald with a stare.

"I'll try. Shoot."

"Turtle Bay *was* an isolated incident. It *was* retribution for a harsh Supreme Court decision here in Coastown. . . . Except for the fact that some Americans were killed, it's a local affair. I don't know if you've read anything about the murders at Fountain Valley golf course on St. Croix—"

"Okay. That theory is all well and good," Peter breaks in. "But what about this blond monkey? Seriously. Can you tell me what a white man was doing there with a sniper's rifle? Kind of gun you use to blow John Kennedy's Adam's apple out with.

Tell me something comforting about that guy and I'll go home happy. Won't bother you ever again."

Brooks Campbell gets up from his desk. He makes a tiny crack in the drapes and bright sunlight pierces into the attic room.

"You know what, Peter?" he says, shrugs, gives just a hint of a slick politician's smile. "I *don't know* what in hell a white man was doing up there.

"Let me tell you a little state secret, though. I've listened to over, oh, fifty people who have *clues* about Turtle Bay. I've listened to the police, the Army . . . and *everything* I've heard so far points to Colonel Dassie Dred. I don't know what else to tell you here, Peter."

Campbell stops his pacing.

His mind has been wandering back to a meeting one year ago in the Nevada desert. To slick projections made about Damian and Carrie Rose.

Christ! They'd screwed up already. Rose was blown wide open. The great, mysterious Damian Rose—*whom even they had never been able to see.*

Campbell looks across the small attic room at Peter Macdonald. His eyes fall to the Hawaiian shirt.

"Trust me, Peter." Campbell smiles half-heartedly, his mind still on the Roses. "Leave my secretary a number where I can reach you."

Peter doesn't answer right away. *Mind going a little crazy on him. In God we trust. All others pay cash, Brooks. . . .* He has the sudden nauseating feeling that he's all by himself again.

"Jesus" slips out of his mouth.

Then the surly black secretary comes back, and the interview is over.

Peter leaves the big white mansion in a sweat. He can't remember feeling so alone and down in a long, long time. Not since the march into Cambodia.

The Season of the Machete

As he walks through the pretty Embassy grounds, he nods at the well-scrubbed Marines on guard duty, smiles at the Walt Disney World tourists—but he keeps thinking back to the government actor, Brooks Campbell.

Who meanwhile stands behind a big dormer window up on the third floor. Smoking a True Blue cigarette, watching Macdonald go out the front gates.

The Witness.

Just before noon, the Loner shuffles down Bath Street in Coastown.

The long-haired man, "Dyno-mite," is holding Carrie Rose's letter as if it's a birthday party invitation his mother has told him to keep nice and clean.

Chackalackus and a cockatoo chat up and down the pretty, quiet side street. A few pariah dogs bark at him and the Loner barks back. Some goats are mindlessly lunching on garbage and scruffy back lawns— and the Loner remembers that he's hungry too.

Also stoned out of his mind. Wasted. Blown away. Feeling rather nice on the balmy afternoon.

No. Fifty Bath turns out to be the office of the *Evening Star* newspaper.

The Loner rings a bell hanging loose by its own electrical wires. Then he waits.

In a few minutes, a black girl with hibiscus in her hair appears in the doorway. The girl is laughing as though she's just been told a joke.

She accepts the manila envelope, and then suddenly,

unbelievably, loud shotgun blasts shatter the quiet of the side street.

The Loner is thrown hard against the doorjamb and wall. His skinny, needle-tracked arms fly up, palms out flat. His hair flies like a dirty mop being shaken out. Bullets hold him against the wall, stitching his chest and face. He's dead before he slides to the ground.

A few minutes later, the *Evening Star*'s flabbergasted black editor is trying to read the letter the man has brought. The letter appears to be from Colonel Dassie Dred—Monkey Dred.

It promises the most severe and unusual punishments if the white foreigners don't leave San Dominica.

It promises that if the letter itself isn't printed for all to see in the evening news, a similar delivery will be made at 50 Bath Street the following morning.

At 12:30, Dr. Meral Johnson arrives at the tiny newspaper office.

The black police chief examines the gaping hole in the newspaper office's front door. He looks at the blown-up dead man. Talks with the young girl who's accepted the letter. Sends his men scouring the neighborhood, trying to find out if anyone has witnessed the shooting.

Then, it's Meral Johnson himself who comes up with the name "Dead Letter" to describe the delivery. Thus far, Dr. Johnson realizes sadly, it's just about his only contribution to the extraordinary case.

The *crème de la crème* of the Intelligence people are the plodding bureaucrats. The worst of them are the Ivy League and Eton boys. And in this case, the *crème* doesn't necessarily rise to the top.

The Rose Diary

Fairfax Station, Virginia

That afternoon and evening, Washington, D.C., is filled with ironic talk about the fall of Saigon. Speechwriters for Gerald Ford are already busy preparing a vow that America will keep its pledges abroad; that America is not turning back to isolationism.

Thirteen miles southwest of the capital, Harold Hill's Old Virginny Home sits on six neat acres in Fairfax Station.

The land is closed in by green, rolling hills and white picket fences. It's rich in honeysuckle, boxwoods, dogwoods, and full-bred domestic animals.

On one of the white fence gates is the hand-painted sign OUR OLD VIRGINNY HOME.

Perhaps! But when Harold Hill is away from home, he sometimes refers to the place as "Vanilla Wafer."

From every vantage point, the Hill homestead seems innocent and indistinctly sweet. The most secretive thing anyone might associate with the normalesque place would be the presence of one of A. C. Nielsen's famous survey TVs.

But never murder, or mayhem, or Intelligence.

Which is more or less the way Harry the Hack wants it.

On most weekday evenings during the spring and early summer, Hill is in the habit of playing hardball with his son, Mark.

Mark is fourteen, a budding star in Babe Ruth League baseball, and every night when there's no game, he has to throw his father one hundred strikes, or be damned.

Hill is haunched awkwardly over loose-fitting Topsiders that night; just sweating nicely; starting to enjoy the exercise—the warm itch in his palm under a Rawlings catcher's mitt.

Suddenly, he's called to the house by his wife, Carole.

"Long Distance calling," Carole shouts from the porch in an Alabama accent she hasn't lost while living in eight different countries. "It's Brooksie Campbell."

Hill excuses himself to his son, then jogs up toward the big Colonial-style house.

On the way inside, forty-four-year-old Harold Hill starts to feel a little turmoil in his stomach.

Brooks Campbell just doesn't call you at home. Not to shoot the bull, anyway . . . And there's something about this terrorism bullshit—Campbell's so-called specialty—that doesn't sit well with Harold Hill anyway.

Terrorism is something for the Arabs and Israelis. Arabs, Israelis, Irish, Symbionese Liberation Army. Something for the little people who *have* to play dirty. Terrorism just isn't something Americans should be getting involved with.

Inside his den, Hill dials an eight hundred number on a phone he keeps in a locked desk drawer.

Now what would happen—he continues his thought from outside—if a major power started playing dirty pool on a regular basis? All-out no-holds-barred dirty? What would happen if America fought a real "guerrilla" war? Shee-it! is what would happen. Return to the Dark Ages.

Hill punches an extension button and the call from the Caribbean is switched onto a safe line, a scrambler.

Outside he can still see Mark.

Throwing up high pop-ups over an old spruce. Catching them basket-style like Willie Mays. The boy has an incredible throwing arm. Incredible.

Just as he begins to think that the telephone switchover is taking too long, he hears Brooks Campbell.

"Hello, Harry." A slightly muffled Campbell—his deep, stage voice a little muddy. "The reason I'm calling, Harry—"

Harold Hill lets out a short, snorting laugh meant to slow down the younger man.

"I think I'm going to sit down for that. For the reason you're calling."

"Yeah, sit down. It's not good news. . . . It turns out, uh, that Rose was seen by a man at Turtle Bay yesterday. How about that? We buy someone *even we haven't seen,* a fucking genius, supposedly, and he's immediately made by somebody else. Shit, Harry. If I didn't know better, I'd say that somebody is fucking around with us. At any rate, I don't want to take any chances with this."

"Does Rose know he was seen? Tell me the whole thing, Brooks."

"Basically he knows his situation," Campbell says. "He called us today. At least his wife did. She says they want to take care of it themselves. Cute?"

"Terrific."

"The man who saw him is a nobody, thank God. American, though . . . By the way, Rose shot and cut up the president of ASTA this morning. Harry, they're free-lancing like crazy now. I don't even remember the original plan we were shown. He skipped a meeting with me last night. They've gone fucking nuts on us."

Harold Hill closes his eyes and visualizes Campbell. Brooks Corbett Campbell. Princeton man. WASP from New London, Connecticut. Slated for big things at the Agency. Neo-Nazi, in Hill's humble opinion. Kind of guy who always thinks he knows what's best for everybody else.

"Well, uhhh . . . I think we have to go along with them a while longer. Don't you? Maybe *you* ought to lay hands on this witness. It seems to me that we may need him to identify Rose. Eventually, anyway . . . I have no intentions of letting them leave the islands after this is over. That's an obvious stroke."

"Sounds good." Brooks Campbell raises his voice above some transatlantic chatter. "That's pretty much the way I see it right now."

Hill pauses for a moment. He thinks he ought to try and cheer Campbell up a bit anyway. SOP.

"All right. Okay on that," says Harry the Hack. "Now let me have the bad news."

Young Brooks Campbell tries to laugh. Your basic combat camaraderie. "Thought you'd never ask," he says.

Coastown, San Dominica

"Let's try to look at this shitty mess logically," Jane suggests.

Peter doesn't answer. He's way off someplace else. At the artillery range outside Camp Grayling in central Michigan. Shooting tin cans off Brooks Campbell's head. With a bazooka.

At ten that night the two of them are out on the dark patio of Le Hut Restaurant. Trying to comprehend mass murder. Occasionally picking through a stew pot of oily bouillabaisse. Both of them about as hungry as the shrimp in the pot.

Peter finally raises his puppy-dog brown eyes to her. Shrugs. "Who could come up with that kind of idea?

. . . Slicing up two nineteen-year-old kids like Jack the Ripper?"

Jane sits with her chin in the palms of thin hands. Serious, she looks like an older version of Caroline Kennedy. She's catching the eye of all the black waiters.

"Probably the same kind of creep who would make two little kids watch their own father die," she answers. "It just makes me feel so awful. Creepy and sick. Really shitty—besides being scared."

Thinking back on the scene at the American Embassy, Peter begins to feel a little useless. Motelike. Little Mac fucks it up again. . . . Maybe he just hadn't explained himself well enough, he thinks. *Something* sure had gone wrong at the Embassy. Because the Tall Blond Man *was* important one way or the other. He had to be.

Jane points out to the street. Playful grin on her face; pre-machete smile.

"I didn't know one of your brothers was down on the island. Heh, heh."

Right in front of Le Hut, a street clown is entertaining a small crowd. The scruffy clown is white. BASIL: A CHILDREN'S MINSTREL his hand-painted sign says.

Basil's a young man behind all his Indian and clown paints. Around the eyes he seems very serious about the show, even a little sad. Only dressed the way he is—raggy canary-yellow pantaloons, an outrageous pastel nightcap—the man also seems pixilated.

"Love is the answer," he says to natives and a few tourists walking past him on Front Street. "Love is the answer," he whispers to the people eating and drinking in Le Hut.

"Ahhh," Jane whispers to Peter, winks, talks like Charlie Chan. "But what is question?"

She sees that he's still partially lost in his own thoughts. Turtle Bay. Whatever had upset him at the U.S. Embassy.

"Do you know any children's tricks? Children's minstrel tricks?" she whispers across the table. "Macduff? Are you there? Are you here with me? Or off solving great murders like Sherlock Holmes?"

Peter smiles and blushes. "Sorry. I'm here. Hello!"

He travels back to the café from faraway places: Vietnam; his parents' house up on Lake Michigan—where every summer for six straight years Betsy Macdonald came and dropped another brown-haired, brown-eyed baby boy. The Super Six.

"Children's tricks?" Peter grins. Has a rush of feeling for this eccentric plains girl from Dakota.

He thinks for just a second. Remembers something his brother Tommy used to do for his kids.

Peter picks up his Le Hut paper napkin. Twists it tight and holds it under his nose.

The napkin looks like a droopy mustache. Greasy. Full of fish scraps.

"You must pay the rent," Peter says in an obvious villain's voice.

He switches the napkin to the side of his hair. It becomes a girl's ribbon. "I can't pay the rent," he says in the falsetto of a heroine in distress.

Mustache voice: "You must pay the rent!"

Ribbon voice: "I can't pay the rent!"

He switches the napkin under his chin where it becomes a puffy bowtie. Peter speaks in a voice like Dudley Do-Right.

"*I'll* pay the rent!"

Ribbon voice: "My hero."

Mustache voice: "Curses, foiled again."

"I wish it was that easy," Jane says.

She kisses his paper mustache. Laurel and Hardy-ha-ha. Neither of them quite full-fledged adults yet.

Not in all ways. Lots of good intentions to grow up, though.

That night they sleep together for the last time. Ever.

Crafton's Pond, San Dominica

Meanwhile, the first meeting between the Roses and Colonel Monkey Dred is close to its very shaky start.

Motors off, four cars sit on opposite sides of a flat, narrow field near Nate Crafton's rat-infested pond in the West Hills District. The field's regular use is for prop planes coming and going to New Orleans with shipments of *ganja* and cocaine.

This particular night, it's misty up around the pond itself. The wet grass is full of long, husky water rats.

By mutual agreement, each side has brought only two cars. There are to be no more than two passengers in either auto. Since there seems to be no way to prevent them, guns have been permitted.

Shortly before starting time, a *third* vehicle appears on the horizon on Dred's side of the field. *At 1:00* A.M.

The first violation of the treaty for this evening.

As Monkey Dred is driven forward in a noisy, British-made van, the twenty-seven-year-old Jamaican-and-Cuban-trained revolutionary sees that the secret airfield is dark, without motion. Quite pretty, with a pale quarter moon set over the surrounding jungle.

The van stops with a jolt at the edge of the field.

Dred's driver flashes his headlights on and off. On and off.

Across the moonlit darkness, another set of car lights flashes on, then off. *Rose*.

Watching the scene through a cloudy, bug-smeared windshield, Dred starts to nod and smile. Rose is already accepting compromises: the *third* car. "Goan to be easy, mon," he says to his driver.

Two of the five cars then drive halfway out onto the landing field. Once again, the agreed-upon procedure. The Roses very keen on orderly procedures, Dred is beginning to notice. Like the British in the American Revolution.

Before his van has fully stopped, the colonel jumps out and stands at rigid attention in the tall grass.

Less than forty yards away, he can see Rose climbing out of some kind of American pleasure car.

The white man isn't as big as Dred has expected. Not bigger than life, certainly. . . . He's wearing a light-colored suit with a big Panama-style hat. Very flashy. Absurdly so.

On signal, the headlights of both vehicles are turned off.

Then the two start to walk toward one another in the dark.

In less than thirty seconds, they're only a few feet apart. The smell of some kind of fertilizer meets that of a strong French cologne.

"Yo' hab dose guns for me?" The revolutionary speaks with a heavy island patois.

Carrie Rose takes off the floppy yellow hat. She smiles at Colonel Dred.

"You're a dead man," she says. "My husband has you in the sights of an M-21 sniper's rifle right now. The rifle has a night sighting device so that he's watching us in a pretty green light. Care to wave?"

"I don't believe dat." The black man remains calm.

Carrie puts her hat back on and a powerful rifle shot kicks up a clod of grass not three feet away from the guerrilla. The lights on all the cars around the field shoot back on again. The black man freezes. Throws a hand up to keep his people in place.

"Our intentions are good." Carrie talks as if nothing at all has happened. "But we wanted you to know that you mustn't try to do anything other than what we agree upon. We agreed on only *two* cars apiece. Not three. Two.

"If you're still interested in guns," the tall woman continues, "you'll come to the Charles Codd estate. Tomorrow evening at ten o'clock. Similar arrangements. *Two* cars."

"Why yo' doin it?" the black man finally asks. He folds his arms; stands his ground.

"We want to help you take over this island," Carrie says to him. She shrugs. "We're being paid to do that. Come to the Codd estate tomorrow. You'll find out everything you want to know. You'll even meet Damian."

Carrie Rose then turns away. She leaves the guerrilla leader a little dumfounded. Beginning to wonder how it happened with Castro up in the Sierra Maestra mountains. Who had come to set him up with guns and bombs?

"He's just a boy," Carrie says to the Cuban as she gets back inside the dark American car. "Isn't that funny that they would be interested in him?"

"Solamente tres días mas" is all the Cuban says.

Just three days more.

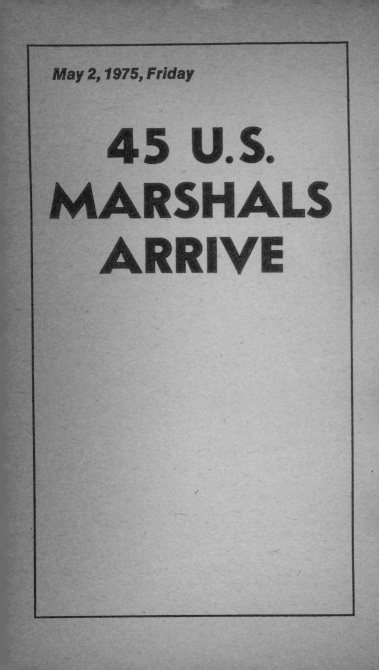

May 2, 1975, Friday

45 U.S. MARSHALS ARRIVE

We'd carefully plotted out a fun-house maze of confusion. Confusion on all fronts. Like a blizzard in summer, where it's never even snowed before. . . .

By May 2, ordinary farmers wielding machetes in their fields stimulated heart attacks. A black man wading in the surf—even an unfamiliar black lifeguard—was enough to send piggy little whites scurrying inside their expensive straw-roofed huts. Fishing boats that drifted too close to shore were waved away by private guards with rifles. *No one shut their eyes sunbathing on the beaches.* . . . And countless tourists spent their sun-time in dingy prop airline and government offices. Pan Am, Eastern, Prin-Air, BOAC, all put on extra flights, but even these couldn't accommodate the exodus. . . . So far, we were pretty much on schedule.

The Rose Diary

The fourth day was much quieter—four island deaths reported. All of them grisly machete murders, however.

Early in the morning, forty-five United States federal marshals were flown in to help keep order in the larger cities of San Dominica. Some of these same State Department marshals had been used during the American Indian uprising at Wounded Knee.

Eight Vietnam-style HSL-1 helicopters came in

from Pensacola, Florida, to help with surveillance and search work.

Because they'd been painted with green and brown combat camouflaging, the helicopters provided one of the scarier sights for the remaining tourists. Suddenly it looked and sounded as if they were in the middle of an undeclared war zone. Army helicopters were continually swooping down out of the lush green hills, looking like the opening scenes in M*A*S*H.

More witnesses to the machete murders were being found too: "a veritable anthology of fascinating, conflicting stories," one French newspaper would eventually say. Five hundred eleven people questioned so far, but no one other than Peter Macdonald claiming to have seen a white man with the raiding parties of blacks.

The chance of Macdonald's story having any effect now seeming rather small, in fact.

There are simply too many chiefs on the scene, too many chiefs prowling around the ghoulish morgues, too many hip experts who think they understand what's going down.

What we did on San Dominica was something like turning loose Charles Starkweather and Carll Fugate, Speck, Bremer, Manson, and Squeaky Fromme. All in one place at the same time.

The Rose Diary

May 2, 1975; Coconut Bay, San Dominica

FRIDAY MORNING, THE FOURTH DAY OF THE SEASON

Lieutenant B. J. Singer, a 1966 Annapolis product, sits in an undersized aluminum beach chair reading a book called *Supership*. His wife, Ronnie, lies beside him with *The Other Side of Midnight* propped up in the sand.

Neither of the Singers is a very enthusiastic reader.

Suddenly *Supership* slips through B. J.'s fingers.

The shiny hardcover book hits the metal arm of the beach chair, then falls broken-backed onto the sand. B. J.'s head drops back.

"What?" Ronnie says.

"I can't stand it." Her husband sits with his eyes closed, with coconut butter glistening all over his body.

"I hate this sitting around. I feel like a goddamn

kid who has to have his mother come with him every time he wants to take a swim or go explore. Or do anything!"

Ronnie Singer looks up from her paperback. She closes one eye to the bright 10:00 A.M. sun.

"Oh, go ahead, then." She talks with the softest, teasing, Texas accent. "You go drown yourself, honey. Get your head cut off by the Zulus. . . . See if Mom really cares. Mom doesn't care a damn."

B. J. crosses one hairless leg over the other. The big red-headed man growls at his wife.

"Ohhh . . . Mom cares," Ronnie then coos from her beach blanket.

"I would like . . . to take off this itchy swimsuit now. On *our* own personal, private beach. And soak up some of *our* own private sun on my own shriveled private parts. And dip those poor neglected bastards in *our* sparkling blue sea. . . . Just like the TV ads suggested. Remember the TV ad for this place?"

Ronnie Singer closes her book with a dull thud. The little blonde woman lets out a large-sized sigh. Her big breasts expand impressively under a thin, polka-dot strip of bathing suit. *Mom,* she calls herself.

"All right, let's go for a walk, sailor."

"I'll do it." B. J. flashes a smile.

"I don't know if I'm brave enough to take off my clothes, though."

"Swish, swish, swish," B. J. kids her.

"Very funny, B. J. Cool it."

The walk north through two pretty coves. To a smaller, more private beach where the big brown hulk of a wrecked schooner sits out a few hundred yards from shore.

When they come up even-steven with the rigless boat, B. J., then Ronnie, wades out into clear, blue-green water full of tiny angelfish.

Ronnie slips off the top of her suit and lets her sand-white breasts float free on the water. She starts to laugh, to blush, even.

Once the cool water gets up around his chest, the Navy man turns to check out the Kelly-green of West Hills.

"Prettiest damn jungle . . ." he starts to say.

Then he sees two shirtless blacks lying in a grove of baby palms. Unbelievable, heart-freezing sight. You never believe it can happen to you.

"Oh, Jesus, my God," he whispers to Ronnie. "They're on this beach."

The young couple begins to swim out toward the shipwreck. Slow wading at first, then an athletic breast-stroke.

"Go behind it." B. J. has taken command. "You make it okay, Ronnie?"

Damian Rose's first rifle shot hits with a *thunk* eight yards in front of them.

The Singers pull up short. Then they keep going toward the old wreck. Much more frantic now. Hard, splashing strokes.

A second shot kicks up water less than a foot away from B. J. A third shot echoes in the distance but never seems to hit anywhere. B. J. doesn't let on that he's been hit in the back.

Then they're in the long, cool shadow cast by the schooner. The boat towering thirty to forty feet over their bobbing heads. Ugly rot and barnacles visible all over the sides.

As they swim around one corner of the schooner, Ronnie feels a strong sweep of water at her side. Like a cold spring.

The topless woman turns her head slightly—sees a four-, maybe five-foot silverish shadow not twelve inches away. For a moment, she stops swimming altogether. Her head dips underwater. She has quick panicked thoughts of her two young sons back in Newport News; of her mother; of drowning.

Another silver streak surfaces at B. J.'s side. Flashing. Twisting. At least a sixty-pound great barracuda. Two of them now.

"Swim easy," B. J. gasps. "Stay behind the boat. No matter what. Swim easy, babe."

The cigar-shaped fish seem to glide in the water. Back and forth with the larger humans; touching them with their tails as if exploring; showing off sharp, pointy teeth.

Feeling the pain in his upper back, B. J. finally floats under the schooner's sagging bowsprit. From there, he can see the beach clearly.

He spots the two barebacked blacks retreating up into the hills. He can't see the rifleman anywhere. . . . He watches the blacks until they disappear into thick jungle. Watches until the pain in his back is too great.

Then he and Ronnie paddle around the boat—a man and a woman—and the two big, surging fish.

The Singers are careful not to make sudden movements as they swim. They're careful to do as little splashing as possible. As little breathing.

And, finally, when the young man and woman get into four or five feet of water—when they can just touch bottom—the great barracudas turn away. The fish flash their tails and head back toward the old wreck. . . . B. J. and Ronnie run the last fifty yards into shore.

And as the Singers lie on the wet sand, like shipwreck survivors, Damian Rose *squeezes, squeezes,* shoots them both dead anyway.

To be simplistic about things, I just didn't want to
live and die in some godforsaken whistle stop.
Like Madame Bovary.

The Rose Diary

Coastown, San Dominica

At eleven o'clock that morning, Carrie Rose lounges
beside a 2,500,000-gallon salt-water swimming pool
at the Coastown Princess Hotel.

Next to her at the pool-side bar, a thirty-three-year-
old stockbroker from New York, Philip Becker, is
lamenting the decline and fall of the good life. He's
also trying to put the make on Carrie.

"It is a sad, shitty affair." Philip Becker eulogizes
San Dominica in a most good-natured way. "Here
you finally *make time* for a vacation. You pay out
two thousand, say, for ten glorious days of *not* having
to schlepp around Manhattan with all the gum-snap-
pers, pan-handlers, the general roll call of sewer
snipes. . . . And then suddenly, *slam-bam,* you don't
just get a little rain to ruin your good times. . . . You
don't get a Solarcaine sunburn. . . . You get a bloody
revolution!"

Carrie shakes out her long sandy hair, exposes the

tiniest mother-of-pearl earrings. She's beginning to smile at the way Becker is telling his dim-witted stories.

"I like the way you say that." She rests her hand on the back of his. " 'You get a revolution!' "

"That is exactly what we have here," the stockbroker says. "Machete knife behind every palm tree."

He's beginning to stare openly at her breasts now; her long legs; brown swimmer's stomach; her crotch.

"This Dred—excuse me, *Colonel* Dred—is going to do some major-league blood-letting now. Which means that I'm going back to the *safer* confines of New York."

"All of a sudden a hundred and fifty thousand tourists and landowners want to get off this island at the same time," Carrie says.

Philip Becker smiles. He raises his glass in a mock salute. "To, uh . . . Colonel Monkey Dred, who, uh, ruined our respective vacations. Up yours, Monkey."

At which point, Carrie Rose decides that she likes this one well enough. Philip Lloyd Becker. A wonderfully confident man. Nearly as smooth as Damian Simpson Rose.

Smooth Philip continues to smile at her. He's gallant. Handsome. Physically nice: a walking advertisement for the New York Athletic Club. And he's empty-headed as the proverbial dizzy blond.

When he finally asks her if she wants to go back to his suite, Carrie says that yes, she does. Very much so.

That's the beginning of a little *cherchez la femme* side plot. Also an experiment.

FRIDAY AFTERNOON

Down and out in Coastown, disoriented as people in a Neil Simon situation, Peter and Jane first get the bum's rush at San Dominica's Government House. Then at the local office of United Press International. Then at the *Gleaner* and the *Evening Star* newspaper offices.

"If, indeed, there is a mysterious white man involved," a British-sounding Uncle Tom at Government House explains, "he'll most surely turn up when we catch Colonel Dred. And, right now, we are *trying* to put all our efforts into catching Dred."

"Well, Jesus Christ, man. Don't let us keep you from the manhunt," Peter says before Jane can pull him away.

At noon, the two of them wander through the crowded Front Street marketplace.

Children are selling green coconuts, yams, fresh fish. Tinny record-shop speakers blast songs like "Kung Fu Fighting." Jane is getting leers and lazy smiles from all the local males.

"Take a taxi ride, lady?"

"Eat me coconut?"

One block off Front Street, they go out onto the very famous and beautiful Horseshoe Beach.

"This could be the nicest day anywhere. Ever," Jane says as they begin to walk on the gleaming sand. "God!"

The entire surface of the Caribbean is nearly white, glittering with the brightest galaxy of stars. Jane's long blond curls are shining. . . . She's the blond beauty you always see at beaches, but nobody ever seems to get.

As the two of them walk along—in spite of their best intentions not to—they begin to feel wonderfully calm and content. As if nothing really matters except the buttery sun, getting a tan, keeping the sea spray in their faces.

"It's so grand, Peter. Kowabunga! Old Indian expression of delight and awe—from the Howdy Doody Show."

"Kind of makes you wonder why somebody would pick central Michigan to settle in. Any cold climate. 'Oh, Caleb, isn't that the most gorgeous stretch of tundra. Let's build our house there.' "

"Oh . . . hush, puppy."

Walking barefoot, carrying their loafers and sandals, they pass under a low wooden pier. Pilings coated with seaweed and barnacles. Some sort of hot sauce and clam bar chattering overhead.

As they emerge from under the dark, rotting planks, Peter happens to glance up at the boardwalk. What he sees snaps his perfect mood like a twig.

Sauntering along, carefree as tourists, are the black killers from Turtle Bay. The Cuban and Kingfish Toone.

Even more disturbing, the smaller of the two is pointing down at the beach. Right at Jane and himself.

"Janie, we don't have time to think this out," he says. "But I want you to get ready to run like an absolute madwoman. The killers from Turtle Bay are at our beach."

Meanwhile the two blacks hurry to a set of wooden stairs twisting down to the sand. Dressed in lightweight suits and fedoras, they look like duded-up Caribbean businessmen.

Peter looks back once and sees the two men running. Strong-looking bastards. Coming like goddamn madmen. Knocking sunbathers down and stepping on them. *What the hell are they figuring on? A public execution?*

"Let's go. Run!"

Split-splat. Split-splat. Bare feet kicking sand high. Kicking sand on people sunbathing on either side of their running track. Jane running good, thank God. Jesus!

Trying to keep up the pace, Peter scrambles for some smart idea of what to do now. He look back over his shoulder again. Almost train-wrecks into a family drag-assing hotel towels.

Finally, he and Jane just start screaming for help. . . . *American sun-dreamers doing absolutely zilch. Backing away from the chase. Kitty Genovese goes to the Caribbean!*

Stumbling through a particularly jammed beach-towel parking lot, Jane can feel her chest and thighs starting to burn up. A slight stitch in her side.

A hundred yards ahead, she spots squat limestone buildings. Showers. Dressing rooms. Shooting from the roof of the little complex, a white stairway to the board-walk.

"Peter! Way up there!"

A few strides farther on, Peter is grabbing the cabana jacket of a tall, very hairy man. "Help us!" he gasps. "Will you call the police?"

The hairy man shoves him. Steps back. "Keep your hands off. Get away from me, you."

Nobody listening. No wonder the police and the U.S. Embassy people have been so strange—they can't believe somebody is trying to help.

Even more terrified, the young man and woman start to run again.

Breaking through crowds heading in to shower and dress in the limestone buildings. Fat boys with plastic footballs. Strong smells of sun lotions. Not really feeling these people hit off their bodies. Numb, everything unreal.

Inside the bathhouse is a large, cool concrete room. No discernible purpose for the room. Twenty or thirty people milling around. Rude Boys smoking corncob pipes. Four different doors going out.

"Stairs?" Peter screams at a pink face under a big straw hat. PRINCESS.

"The stairs!" Jane screams with him now. "Tell us where!"

As PRINCESS points left, Peter and Jane hear a commotion starting up behind them.

Suddenly a black lifeguard runs out of one of the concrete hallways. O. J. Simpson with corn locks. He yells in a booming voice at the two men just coming through the main entrance.

Booooomm!

A single, unbelievable explosion echoes through the bathhouse. Bright red blood sprays all over. The shocked lifeguard crashes back into a limestone wall. He comes off the wall face first, braids jangling, down onto the concrete floor.

All kinds of people screaming "Murder!" in the strange, bare room. People diving on the floor . . . A hole as big as a baseball in the lifeguard's back. Red Rorschach splatter. Total panic.

Peter and Jane off and running again. Feeling shitty

about the young black guy. *Left*—but they don't see any stairs left.

"You got any ideas?"

"No."

"Holy shit."

Another wild-mouse left and they find doors. BATHROOM, MEN'S SHOWER, CLOSET, WOMEN'S SHOWER, MAINTENANCE. Then they're at a complete dead end in the building. Fresh out of clever ideas too.

Then Jane gets her idea. "Here."

Inside WOMEN'S SHOWER, billowing steam hits them like a sudden hot fog. They see the bare rump of a white woman. Two rumps. Rows of gray lockers and benches.

"Look for someplace to hide in here."

The bare woman goes left, Peter and Jane right. As they do—dragging one another around sharp locker corners—they hear the big metal door to the corridor open and shut again.

"Nice try anyway," Peter says.

He yanks at a wooden door and they're inside a narrow tiled room with five or six showers running water. Down through the waterfalls, they see a naked black woman and a little girl of about three.

The girl has a head full of creamy soap suds. She's looking at the strange, intruding white couple as if they're the real Laurel & Hardy. The girl's mother looks terrified, though. Hands across her breasts. Starting to scream.

"Please," Jane whispers, walking right back through the showers, dragging Peter. "I know how it must look, but men are chasing us. Please don't scream."

At the end of the showers, the two of them slip into a narrow alcove.

"Hidden from the front door, at least."

"What do yo' want in here?" The black woman finally speaks to them.

"Please help us," Jane whispers again.

Pressed unbelievably hard against the damp tile wall, feeling her much cooler perspiration mix with the warm shower-room water, she has an image that makes her tremble. A clear picture of the two men coming into the shower. Firing at her and Peter. Firing at the woman. Firing at the little girl. BIZARRE SHOWER-ROOM MASSACRE!

They can all hear the two men outside in the dressing rooms. Loud voices. Curses. Women screaming. Lockers slamming and opening.

"I think I'm having a nosebleed," Jane says.

Then it doesn't matter. Nothing does. The two killers are inside the shower room.

Thinking about hand-to-gun combat, Peter listens to the black woman.

"What do you want in here?" she says to the two men. The same thing she'd asked him and Jane.

Neither of the Turtle Bay killers answers her either. Then a man's shoes click down hard against the tile floor. Cleats. Coming back to check for himself. So weird not being able to see the bastard. Gun drawn?

Every muscle in both Peter and Jane's bodies begins to clench. Across from them a wet mop is leaning against the wall. Weapon? . . . *Weapon*.

Peter feeling unbelievably protective suddenly. Full of rage. Ready to hit the black butcher boy with the mop. Make a try for his gun. One shot at the guy in the front. Impossible odds.

Then the second man calls out. Something in Spanish. *Vamonos*.

Both men leave the room, and there's immediately screaming outside. More doors slamming.

Jane hangs up on the wall like a wet tissue. Blond hair down and dirty like a mop. Her nose bleeding.

Peter sinks down to a full squatting position. Fetal position. Scared shitless position.

Peter sees that the black woman in the shower with them is quite young. Twenty. Twenty-one. All ribs and sharp bones.

The little girl is very, very pretty. Crying now because her mother is crying.

"Jesus, we're sorry," Peter says.

He and Jane wait a few minutes, make the woman promise to tell the story to the police, then they leave the dressing room.

Out in the concrete halls they don't see either of the black killers. The building is jammed with people, though. Unbelievable shouting is blasting up and down the concrete tunnels. People are crying.

Finally, they find the stairway out. They push and shove their way through a wide-eyed crowd trying to find out what's happened. *"Is it another machete murder?"* . . . At the top of the stairs, Jane grabs Peter hard around his chest. "Hold me, Peter," she says. "Just hold me for a minute."

Then, for the second straight day, the police of San Dominica take descriptions of the Cuban and Kingfish Toone.

"No blond Englishman?" the constable asks.

"He was there," Peter says. *"We just didn't see him this time."*

The black policeman smiles. "WE didn't see him last time either."

Las Vegas, Nevada

FRIDAY EVENING

That night in Las Vegas, the whole San Dominica operation continues toward a major blowup at breakneck speeds: Great Western Air Transport reestablishes contact with the Forlenza Family for the first time since Lathrop Wells.

At ten o'clock, a long-haired fat man—somebody's bright idea of a professional gambler type—follows Isadore Goldman's chauffeur-driven Fleetwood out of the glittering Flamingo Hotel. Toward "Downtown."

The fat Intelligence man's name is Tommie Hicks, and he's a 1968 Stanford Law School graduate. Beyond that, he'd been one of the original CIA representatives at the farmhouse in Lathrop Wells.

Hicks follows Goldman two cars back down Sahara Boulevard. Into the Strip proper. Past 9:58—83 degrees on the Sahara clock. Past the Sands and three hundred other gaudy hotels.

To Caesar's Palace.

Once ensconced inside the gambling mecca, Izzie Goldman begins to play high-stakes blackjack. The old man is what the croupiers call a George player: a very classy high-roller.

In his first hour at blackjack, Goldman wins a comfortable year's salary for most people—just over $34,000. Then, the old man proceeds to lose over $40,000 playing baccarat.

Since Tommie Hicks makes $28,000 a year himself, the turnaround fascinates the hell out of him. Several times during the evening he fantasizes walking up and taking away the old gangster's chips for safe-keeping.

Just after 1:00 A.M., Goldman finally gets up from his chair at baccarat. He heads for one of the men's rooms.

CAESARS it says on the swinging door.

Tommie Hicks follows Goldman one swing behind. He understands perfectly well that he is no more than a centurian in this particular game.

The CIA man takes the shiny urinal to the left of the old man.

Funny thing—Tommie Hicks finds that he doesn't have to go. Not a drop. Kind of humorous actually. Something slightly ludicrous about sleuthing a five-foot-two, seventy-five-year-old man anyway.

"Didn't I meet you at one of Harry Hill's parties?" he asks as the old man tinkles.

A black man—pimp—looks their way from three urinals down the line. The black stud smiles big ivory-and-gold teeth.

Izzie Goldman stares over at Hicks. He shrugs his small, rounded shoulders.

"Not me, Abe."

The old gangster finishes his duty and zips up. He walks over to the fancy sinks. Chewing on a soggy cigar, pushing his gold watch up on his skinny arm, Goldman starts to wash his hands.

The pimp splashes on some English Leather. Then

he walks out of the bathroom without washing his hands.

"Schvuggs like the smell of it." Goldman nods at the closing door. He puts both hands up to his head, seems to be stretching the neat part in his white hair.

"Mr. Hill has a problem, I take it."

"Not so much Mr. Hill. There's a problem with our other two friends."

Isadore Goldman hits the wooshing faucets. He vaguely remembers this fat cow from the farmhouse in the desert.

"A little problem, I hope."

"So far, very little . . . But we want your approval to get rid of both of them if the problem continues."

Goldman squints at himself in the water-spotted mirror over the sink. Prune, he thinks. Small prune, but prune.

He shrugs his shoulders at the younger man standing behind him.

"You should know enough not to ask me. . . . But I'll tell you one thing to make your trip out here worthwhile. I would be very surprised if clever people like these Roses couldn't handle any little problems that come up."

Tommie Hicks smiles in the gilded mirror over the old man's head. "We were very surprised," he says, "that some problems *did* come up."

Turtle Bay, San Dominica

At eight o'clock that night, Macdonald steps off a sputtering, wheezing double-decker bus heading north from Coastown.

Sweat-stained alligator shirt thrown over his shoulder, he starts down the neatly raked gravel driveway of the Plantation Inn.

Having persuaded Jane to stay with friends in Coastown for the night, he's all alone with the problem of being an unwanted only witness.

Apparently, the local police aren't going to help. . . . The people at the U.S. Embassy aren't exactly rolling out the red carpet for him either. . . . Neither are the newspapers.

Why not? That's the $64,000 question. Why the hell not?

Plowing across the dark, deserted Plantation Inn beach front, Peter starts to wonder if all real-life crime investigations might be just as frustrating as this one. A lot of bungling around in the dark. Dumb-bunny screw-ups all over the place. No quick solutions. Not ever.

As he sees the outline of the beach cottage where he

and Jane live, his mind leaps back to the two black killers in Coastown. If those two were home-grown revolutionaries—Dred's people—then he's Cary Grant II.

Paranoid now—careful, anyway—he stops walking.

His heart starts to pound in a way it hasn't since the day he left the lonely hill country of South Vietnam.

From the cover of thick-leaved banana trees, he studies the silent black world like a Special Forces sergeant. . . .

Little pink honeymoon bungalow. Shadowy roof. Louvered windows. Wooden door looking like it had been put up crooked because of the shifting sand. Dark, spooky Caribbean. Nice spot for an ambush . . .

After watching the place for a good ten minutes, seeing no apparent trouble, nothing moving except dark palm fronds and cirrus clouds, Peter begins to walk toward his home.

Halfway up the pebble-and-sea-shell walk, he sees a dark shape thrown across a white patio table.

Moving a step closer, he recognizes Max Westerhuis' afghan and he moans out loud. . . . The beautiful, long-haired dog has been cut in half.

The machetes.

"Oh, Jesus God," he swears out loud. Trembles. Nearly gets sick. It's the first time he's actually seen the work of the razor-sharp knives.

The body of the thoroughbred dog—Fool's Hot Toast—has been separated cleanly across its thin rib cage.

Ants and black flies are eating at the bloody crease like a long, horrifying serving table.

Peter hurries past the dog and goes inside.

First he catches his breath. Then he collects clothes, money, a Colt .44 pistol hidden away in his T-shirts. His personal *memento mori.*

All he can think to do now is hide. Decide whom he

can talk to about whatever is happening. Maybe figure
out a way to get off San Dominica altogether.

Most of all, he wants to lead them away from Jane.
Make it clear to them that their problem is with him.
The Witness.

Wondering why they've gone to the bother of killing
the dog, wondering if they're watching him, and who
the hell the Blond Man is anyway—Peter Macdonald
jogs back toward the brightly lit inn.

He passes quickly through the portico—back into the
dark rear parking lot. He calls Jane in Coastown. Gets
no answer at her friend's.

And then, at 8:45 on May 2—having damn little
idea what he plans to do with it—Peter steals the hotel
manager's BMW motorcycle for the second time that
week.

As he slowly, quietly, rides the bike up the drive, a
tall man steps into the shadowy road now filling up
with dust.

Damian Rose watches Macdonald get away—and
he lets him.

Peter Macdonald is right about on schedule.

Everything is.

The machetes are every bit as effective as he thought
they'd be that first afternoon at Turtle Bay.

If there was any doubt that he and Carrie were
worth $1,000,000 going into the operation, there
wouldn't be after it was over. The two of them are going to be as famous as Charles Manson and Company
—and marketable to boot.

DECLARE WAR ON MONKEY DRED

On the fifth day, San Dominican Prime Minister Joseph Walthey held an emotional press conference to announce that the terrible machete murders could now definitely be attributed to Colonel Dred and his very small group of dissidents.

Standing before news microphones with his wife, with the U.S. ambassador and his wife, Joseph Walthey revealed that at seven o'clock that morning, a battalion of San Dominican and U.S. troops had entered the jungles of West Hills. A confrontation with Colonel Dred was expected before the end of the day.

In the meantime, both Robert F. Kennedy Airport in Coastown and Kiley Airport in Port Gerry had been transformed into angry beehives of abnormal activity.

A spokesman for the airlines said that even at the accelerated flight departure rate, it would take at least another four days to accommodate all of the people who wanted to leave San Dominica, the Virgin Islands, Jamaica, and Haiti.

Small curiosity. While thousands were departing from the islands, a few hundred rabid ambulance-chasers arrived to witness the machete Terrors.

During the first four days, over 250 people came to San Dominica to witness the bizarre scene. Simply to be there. To watch death in action. Maybe even to get a photograph or a sound track.

"I have no moral reactions any more," Damian says. "Sometimes, though, I feel a kind of icy, grand compassion."

The Rose Diary

May 3, 1975; West Hills, San Dominica

SATURDAY MORNING, THE FIFTH DAY OF THE SEASON

Peter is beginning to get his second worm's-eye view of those sneaky, dirty little wars that had come of age—or at least back into vogue—during the 1960s.

For a terrifying few minutes, he has a pretty clear vision of man's inhumanity to man.

Of the bizarre contrivances some men will use to gain an advantage. The horror of being alone and unknowing in the middle of terrorism and guerrilla warfare. Of being an absolute nobody in the greater scheme of things. A zero on the world's Richter scale. A gook.

A thick, dark liquid is dripping dead-center on his chest.

Motor oil, he realizes after a few fuzzy-eyed seconds.

A train is coming!

A train getting close to his hiding place in the West Hills jungle. Colonel Dred's turf.

A train? Peter considers. *Hiding place? He is going buggy.*

He rolls over sideways and peeks through reeds of tall grass; tries to clear his sore throat of pollen and dew.

Two lizards walk by at his eye level, one following the other. They seem to be well acquainted. To be good friends, maybe lovers . . . The two lizards stop and play in the grass like small dinosaurs. Quite gregarious little monsters. Red bubbles throbbing under their green and blue chins.

Macdonald slowly rolls out away from the BMW.

Sits in the grass picking grass and stones out of his arm. Watching the sun peek through trees dripping heavy moss. The sky is flaming overtop of the leaf cover. Hot hot, today.

Hiding out, he considers once again, trying the feeling out like a new sports coat. *On the run.*

After another minute massaging hopeless thoughts, Peter gets up and starts to make a fire. Gathers leaves and a few sticks, twigs, grass reeds, anything dry.

He goes over to the motorcycle and pulls out the German's dandy cross-country kit. . . . In a few minutes, he's making instant Nescafé coffee. Powdered eggs. Some kind of dried, salty beef.

Crouched over the small fire, the young man gulps down the equivalent of four eggs, the worst coffee he can imagine, mystery meat, and a chocolate bar that's come all the way from West Germany *chust for such an occashun.*

While he finishes the quick meal, Peter thinks about Jane. He considers going into Coastown to get her. Decides against it . . . She's better off as far away from him as possible. Probably as far away from the San Dominican police as possible too. For the moment, Jane is fine where she is. Which is more than he can say for himself.

After he finishes breakfast, he goes back into the

BMW's shiny black-leather saddlebags. He takes out a West Point T-shirt and unwraps the Colt .44.

It seems strange, unreal, just holding the old gun. He turns the chamber and sees all eight shells.

Examining the gun further, he remembers Army shooting ranges at West Point—hidden in massive gray-stone buildings on a hill above the football field, Michie Stadium. He remembers a seedy shooting range inside a steaming tin-roofed building in the Cholon section of Saigon.

Peter slowly raises the long-barreled Colt.

Aims it at a mottled banana-tree leaf. Aims at a tiny, chattering yellow bird. Aims at a small green coconut. Finally at a small black snake slithering up a gommier tree.

The tree is a good thirty-five paces away. Thirty-five yards. What pistol enthusiasts regard as trick or show-boat shooting.

Looking like an old-fashioned duelist, aiming ever so carefully, Peter squeezes the trigger gently.

The distant, hard skull of the black snake explodes as if it were rotten inside. The rest of the snake drops from the gommier like a loose vine.

In a way, the neat shot pleases and surprises him.

He really hadn't expected the showpiece pistol to be so well balanced. As for the shooter—well, he knows all about the shooter.

"Hoo boy!" Peter says out loud to the *deangerous* West Hills. "Now what, hotshot?"

The John Simpson Roses. Strange, blue-blood family. Damian's fourteen-year-old brother was caught cheating on a biology exam at the Horace Mann School. Teen-ager swallowed half a beaker of sulphuric acid. Didn't die because the dose was so high he vomited it all up. He was crippled from his neck down, though. In an institution ever since. Damian's mother living in an institution year-round too. Father rides round and round Manhattan and London in a big black limo provided by a multinational bank. Damian planning to kill his father in the limo one day. . . .

                                          The Rose Diary

Mercury Landing, San Dominica

SATURDAY AFTERNOON

The shoreline at Mercury Landing is pretty and very secluded.

Black cliffs rise up high on either side of a sliver of gleaming white sand.

There's a glen of royal palm trees. Yellowbirds. Flocks of parrots like an open-air pet store. A big red sun over the sea like God's angry eye.

There is a big white house over the sea too. And on one side of the house, a dark green sedan is hidden in the shadows of casuarina trees.

There can be no doubt about one thing: San Dominica is a paradise on this earth.

Down on the beach at Mercury Landing a man and woman are walking in the nude.

Without her clothes on, Carrie Rose's legs seem a little too long, a little bowed. Her feet are slightly too large and too flat.

These are nit-picks, however, because the slender young woman is quite beautiful without clothes.

Walking beside her, Damian is almost as impressive to look at. The tall blond man wears nothing, but he has an expensive terry-cloth jumpsuit draped over one arm. He has broad shoulders and well-muscled legs. A hard, flat stomach. Pretty blond hair.

A long, sun-tanned cock hangs out of the light, curly hair between Damian's legs.

"The killing should all be over now," Carrie is saying to him, a little Midwestern twang always in her voice. "It's taking too long, Damian. A week is too long."

Damian just smiles at her. He glances out at a boat coming over a distant reef. A gray smudge on a wiggly black line.

"You just want the tension you're feeling to be over," he says in a soft, detached voice. "It isn't taking too long at all. It's perfect so far. This island is insane and paranoid as a madhouse. . . . Besides, in two days or so you get to leave. You can even start to spend all our money. Buy yourself a few cars or something, Carrie."

Carrie Rose slips her arm around her husband's firm waist.

"I want you to leave with me. I think it will be better that way. Will you do that, Damian? Leave with me."

"If I leave then"—Damian starts to raise his voice—"Campbell and Harold Hill will come looking for us. Sooner or later they'll find us. Suddenly a big black car will arrive at our villa somewhere or other. Their short-haired killers will come down on us like little

Nazis. Kill us. Become heroes. Write books and make movies like *The French Connection*.

"Look at how it's growing." Damian suddenly changes moods, smiles unexpectedly. "Irreverent little beast. *Big* beast."

As he's been talking, his penis has extended itself straight out and to the left. Blood has gone to its head —which is just touching Carrie's bare leg.

She pushes it away.

"If I have to tell you everything explicitly, I'm frightened this time. You're playing too many games this time. I don't want us to end like this. . . . You mentioned little Nazis before. Well, we're going to be searched for like little Nazis."

Damian throws his arms up like a Frenchman. "Let them search. Let them search. They looked for Eichmann for twenty years. They're stupid, Carrie. Remember that. They are all stupid, bumbling idiots."

Carrie just bows her head. It's useless to talk with him when he gets like this. She lets her long hair swing from side to side, brushing over her breasts.

For the next few minutes they walk along the lip of the cove in silence.

"If I were to lie down in the water there?" She finally speaks . . . .

The two beautiful people walk to where the white sand is slicked-over wet.

Damian sets down the expensive terry-cloth suit and Carrie lies on it.

Damian kneels over her—hangs—begins to lower himself slowly. For a fleeting moment, his clear blue eyes seem almost gentle to her.

"So tell me, Carrie," he says. "How was your handsome stockbroker?"

SATURDAY EVENING

The main *coup de théâtre* is staged that night, Saturday, May 3.

At eleven o'clock, automobile headlights appear at Mercury Landing's high, silver-painted front gates.

Emerging from the shadowy gates, the Cuban waves the first car on.

Standing at the other end of the driveway, Damian Rose can hear gravel being crushed under heavy automobile tires.

One hour late, but they're coming anyway.

The Tall Blond Man checks a Smith & Wesson revolver under his suit jacket. A small, snub-nosed .38. A very appropriate weapon for the evening's performance, Rose thinks. . . . Tonight, he's going to play Hammett for the locals.

As he continues to watch down the hill, a second and third set of headlights turn onto the pitch-black driveway.

One pair of lights is outrageously cross-eyed. It exposes tall Bermuda grass on one side of the car. Palm trees and purplish sky on the other.

The three cars completely disappear for a moment. They pass behind bay trees and fire-of-the-forest, where six local gunmen have been told to wait. Just wait.

Then bright headlights spray all over the vined walls and windows of the whitewashed main house. The cars begin to park in a glen of casuarinas in front of the villa.

Ready or not, Damian thinks to himself, this is it. *Curtain time.*

He rehearses all his lines one final time before he has to go on.

Out on a large flagstone terrace at the rear of the villa, Kingfish Toone can be heard speaking pidgin English with a French-Congolese accent.

"We are prepare to offer you cash only," the broad-shouldered mercenary explains to the four guerrilla leaders who've just arrived. "One hundred twenty-five thousand. You could buy whatever you like with the money. Guns. Whatever you like. That is my final offer, Colonel."

Dassie "Monkey" Dred lets his pretty chocolate face fall between his long legs. His long corn-locks fall. He begins to laugh in a loud, crude voice.

Then he starts making bird noises out on the terrace.

"Ayeee! S'mady take dis monkey-mahn away fram me," Dred says to no one in particular. "Dis Africahn smell lak hairdresser fram Americah."

Kingfish Toone smiles along with Dred's men. The African has met and dealt with this type of madman before.

Across the terrace, the Cuban sits in a small wicker rocking chair, saying nothing at all.

"That smell is something called soap. You've never smelled soap before, have you?"

A tall white man speaks from the doorway leading back into the house.

His blond hair is all wet, slicked back close to the scalp. Like something out of *Esquire* or *Gentlemen's Quarterly*.

He's wearing an expensively tailored cream gabardine suit. Appropriate accouterments, perfectly matched. An inlaid ivory watch. An ivory ring. A black Gucci belt and Gucci loafers.

Damian Rose runs his hand back over his wet hair once again.

Then he crosses the patio to the young, bearded revolutionary. As he walks, his jacket swings open revealing a fancy belt holster and the Smith & Wesson.

"Colonel Dred." Damian smiles like a Clint Eastwood character. "Your work is admired far off this island. In Europe, I'm talking about. In black America."

The guerrilla soldier's face softens for a split second that isn't lost on Rose. Then Dred dismisses the compliment with a wave of his hand. He spits on the terrace.

"Yo' very well-train ape"—he indicates Kingfish Toone sitting across the terrace—"has offered me— what is it?—cash. . . . I don't need dat. I have all kind cash from *ganja* sellin'."

Rose's soft blue eyes never leave the much darker eyes of the San Dominican.

"First of all, my 'well-trained ape' could rip off your coconuts in about five seconds' time, Colonel. Secondly, whatever your problem is, we can find a solution."

"He wants the guns used in this raid." The Cuban speaks in Spanish from his seat across the terrace. "He has trouble buying guns."

"For obvious reasons." Damian turns back to Dred. "I don't want to arm you that well, Colonel. . . . You may have the guns, however. We'll give you two hundred fifty M-sixteens. Plus handguns."

"Fifty t'ousan' rounds of ammunition. At least fifty machine guns," Dred shouts. His three officers smile and clap their hands like Barnum and Bailey chimps.

The lips of the tall blond man part in a slight smile. He slides his hands back over the wet hair again. He takes out a pack of English cigarettes.

"I can't give you the machine guns," Damian says flatly.

Suddenly, Monkey Dred is on his feet shouting at the top of his lungs. His corn-locks shake like a hundred dancing black snakes. A U.S. Army ammunition belt around his waist jounces and jangles.

"Forty machine guns, den! Deliver at least one day before dat *massacree*."

Damian Rose picks up a camphor candle from a patio table. He lights his cigarette with it.

The word "massacree" rolls over his tongue. *Massacree.*

"One fifty-millimeter machine gun. For you!" Rose lets the cigarette dangle. "But the other guns to be distributed *right now*. Plus a bonus of twenty-five thousand rounds of ammunition . . . If I could offer you more, I would. It's not my money, Colonel. . . . Our friends in Cuba know what you need, and what you don't."

A loud laugh comes up from somewhere deep in the black man's chest. "All right, den!" he shouts.

Damian Rose smiles. Friends in Cuba, indeed . . . He's won. *Massacree!*

He heaves the red jar and camphor candle far down the hillside toward the Caribbean.

The lamp hits a distant, invisible rock. It breaks with the *pop* of a light bulb.

Just after it hits, lights flash on and off down on the water.

A small motor boat starts to come in toward shore. *Carrie.*

"Your guns, Colonel," Damian Rose announces. "Enough guns and ammunition to take over the entire island . . . if you'll listen to just a bit of advice."

May 4, 1975, Sunday

PRINCESS, SPICE POINT, HIT

As early as 6:00 A.M. *on the sixth day, there were bold, unnerving machete murders in the two most expensive hotels in San Dominica's two principal cities.*

In Coastown, a young fashion photographer from Greenwich, Connecticut, was found floating face down in a pretty courtyard swimming pool in the Princess Hotel. A black-handled sugar-cane machete was sticking out of the man's back like an exclamation point to the crime.

In Port Gerry, an English barrister's wife was hacked to bits and pieces while she was gathering hibiscus in the garden of the exclusive Spice Point Inn.

The woman was then bundled up in Spice Point towels, and thrown onto the inn's dining veranda by fleeing, half-naked black men.

Also very early in the morning, both the Gleaner *and the* Evening Star *received Dead Letters. In these new communications, Colonel Dred claimed responsibility for the morning's hotel murders.*

Dred also warned that the rate of race killings on San Dominica would escalate by 1000 percent daily until an interest in all hotels, restaurants, and other major businesses was turned over to the people.

Someone at the Gleaner *calculated that since four people had died so far on the fourth, a minimum of forty people had to die on May 5.*

Then four hundred . . . Then four thousand . . .

We're conditioned to expect things to happen at a certain rate. To have a certain rhythm. What we did on San Dominica was to take all of the prevailing rhythms away.

The Rose Diary

May 4, 1975; Coastown, San Dominica

SUNDAY MORNING, THE SIXTH DAY OF THE SEASON

At 7:15 the morning of the sixth day, Peter Macdonald steps through the kitchen door of Brooks Campbell's expensive villa in Coastown, shouts, "Scrambled eggs!," and knocks the handsome CIA man down with a hard, right-handed punch to his Greco-Roman nose.

"You better stay right down there," Peter yells as Campbell tries to push himself to his feet.

He takes out the Colt .44 and points the barrel at an imaginary target, one-half inch in circumference, centered between Campbell's hazel-brown eyes.

"What the hell do you want?"

"Just the truth," Peter says quietly. "I'm not going to go into what's happened to me since the last time you fucked me over—how I came to sleep in your garage last night—but I want to know everything you know about the machete murders. I want to know all your so-called state secrets."

Very slowly, cautiously, Campbell gets to his feet in the kitchen.

"There's only one problem with what you're saying," he says to Peter. "I just don't believe you'd shoot me. I know you wouldn't."

The next thing Brooks Campbell sees is the big, steel handle of the Colt .44. It strikes him sideways across the cheekbone and he crashes down on the yellow tile floor again.

"You *will* believe I'll shoot you in a minute," he hears dimly. A brown work boot stamps down hard on his chest, then he's being pulled up roughly by his hair.

Suddenly, he feels a hot streak going down the right side of his face.

"Now, dammit, you better talk to me, mister. I know how to do shit like this. Torturing men. Believe me I do."

Campbell is beginning to focus in on the speed heat burner of his own kitchen stove. The coil is red hot—a glowing orange—and his hair is starting to smoke. Bacon cooking on another burner is spitting all over the other side of his face.

"I swear to God I'll fry your goddamn ear!" Macdonald yells at him, Army drill-instructor style.

"We know the Mafia is involved somehow!" Campbell finally screams out. "Let me up. I'm burning. I'm burning, Macdonald!"

Peter loosens his strangle hold, but not so much that Campbell can get up. "I don't know what that's supposed to mean. The Mafia . . . the Mafia what?"

"They've been trying to get the Assembly here to legalize casino gambling for years. . . . Now they're going to get what they want—or they say they'll destroy this place. Blow up San Dominica and write it off as a tax loss . . . That's all we know. I swear it. Macdonald, I'm on fire!"

Peter finally lets go of Campbell. What he's heard starts to make a little sense. It explains some of the things that have happened.

"What does Colonel Dred have to do with that? With the Mafia? Casino gambling?"

The CIA man is holding his ear as if it's been bitten into. He's wearing a gold-and-red dragon kimono, and for once in his life, Brooks Campbell looks ridiculous.

"We don't know how or even *if* they got to Dred." He continues to tell half-truths with some conviction. "Apparently, something big is coming up soon. Those letters in the newspapers are actually warnings to the Assembly. Some big horror show is coming. What you don't understand is that we're all going wild trying to stop it from happening."

"I'm getting a feeling that you're lying again," Peter says. He opens up the refrigerator and looks around inside. He throws Campbell some ice for the bruise on his face. Then he takes a long, sloppy swig of orange juice from an open jug.

"All right." He waves the cowboy pistol at Campbell. "This has been a little better than our first talk, I guess. I'll be back if I need to know anything else from you. Just don't ever make the mistake of thinking that I wouldn't shoot you. I'd shoot you. I don't even like you."

Peter backs out the kitchen door, then runs to the BMW.

Now what kind of horror show could be coming up? he wonders as he eases the motorcycle down palm-lined lanes, back out toward the rain forest. Would the Mafia get mixed up in something like this? And how does the Blond Man fit in? A mercenary? To do what?

But, Christ, this is a hell of a lot better than being

a bartender for a nutty German storm trooper. . . .
Maybe he has to go become a cop or a Philip Mar-
lowe–type detective or something. Someday soon . . .

After his success with Campbell, Peter is at least
feeling alive again. That's a start.

Coastown, San Dominica

A sea gull flaps up Parmenter Street. Dips to scrutinize natives setting up a brightly colored fruit mart. Angles right shoulder, wing first, and glides like a clever wooden airplane over the exclusive crimson-roofed Coastown Princess Hotel.

Sitting pretty with a big supply of steaming coffee, kipper and eggs, fresh rolls and sweet butter, Carrie Rose is out on her loggia at the Princess.

She's just beginning to compose a long, personal entry in the million-dollar diary.

When she writes, she tells about a particular late-summer afternoon in Paris. An afternoon that had provided a key to the whole thing.

August 10, 1974; Paris

The place was called Atlantic City, and it was a trendy little bistro recently sprung up as a haven for Americans on the Avenue Marceau.

The café was already famous for its twelve varieties

of *le hamburger*. And, to a lesser extent, for its big wooden posters illustrating different trivial points about a seedy boardwalk resort in southeastern New Jersey.

DID YOU KNOW THAT? . . .

THE FIRST EASTER PARADE IN AMERICA WAS HELD IN ATLANTIC CITY. . . .

THE FIRST FERRIS WHEEL WAS OPERATED IN ATLANTIC CITY. . . .

THE FIRST MOTION PICTURE WAS MADE IN ATLANTIC CITY. . . .

THE FIRST PICTURE POSTCARDS WERE FROM ATLANTIC CITY. . . .

Floppy white hat covering half of her face, Carrie Rose walks back slowly into the dark bar. She hears "Lady Marmalade" playing on the juke box. *"Voulez-Vous Coucher Avec Moi?"*

White butterfly stockings swishing softly, she continues until she sees the wheelchair.

Then Carrie realizes that for the first time in a long time, she's frightened.

"The incomparable, infamous Mrs. Rose." Nickie Handy speaks to her from the corner of a candlelit booth. "Now what could your pleasure be this lovely, shitty afternoon?"

As Carrie slides into the oaken booth, she kisses the top of Nickie's head. Her ex-partner. Then, as she settles in across from her old friend, she can't help staring at the little crippled man's face.

Nickie Handy, still not thirty years old, has no left cheek now. No left side to his face. Just sagging flesh hanging off a cheek-bone.

"I should come see you more than this," she says softly. "Both Damian and I are rats, Nickie. We really are bad."

A waitress comes and Carrie orders a bottle of

Pouilly-Fuissé. Nickie makes a remark about the French girl's breasts. "Sow's teats," he says with a crooked little smile.

"Let's have it. Let's have it." He turns back to Carrie. "Don't hand me this visiting-the-local-VFW crap. Buying your hot-shit wines and all that. . . ."

"All right. I came to talk to you about the shooting. Saigon."

A surprised look drops over Nickie Handy's sad, Quasimodo face.

"Let's not," he says. Then suddenly his face twists up like a pretzel and he raises his voice.

"You're looking at me like a fucking cat, Carrie. That disdainful look Siamese cats get. Bee-utiful! I love it, you cunt."

"You're paranoid." Carrie continues to speak softly, almost lovingly. "Damian and I are doing a job with Harold Hill. Harry the Hack and your *very good friend* Brooks Campbell. Who would you suggest we go talk to?"

The cripple takes his mug of beer and slowly spills it out onto the pine and sawdust floor.

"Bee-utiful!"

"Hey! Hey! Hey!" a dark-bearded French bartender calls back. "Behave yourself, Nickee!"

Handy screws up his face again. Some kind of awful tic, apparently.

"Brooks Campbell was supposed to be paying me in that alley in Saigon. Blew my head off instead. 'Hello, Nick.' *Blam! Blam! Blam!* . . . Left me for a fucking cold stiff in the sewer, Carrie.

"Dead chink mouse floated past my nose. I thought I was in hell already. Crippled in the sewer. Face messed up like it is. *Your new partners, you say?*"

"There was no provocation for what they did, Nickie? Privateering? . . . It was just a double cross?"

"Straight double cross! Me and a poor gook bas-

tard. I think he even kept my money for himself.
Brooks Campbell. Fucking movie-star face."

"Those awful bastards, Nickie."

"Your partners," Nickie says again. "I love it! I
love it!"

Carrie and the crippled man sit drinking in the
Americanized bar until after five o'clock.

At that point, American business types begin to
crowd inside. Tourists and backpacking hippies come
from the nearby L'Etoile.

By 5:30, it's impossible to hear a normal conversation inside the tacky bistro.

Saying something about cigarettes, Carrie goes inside her shoulder bag. She then reaches over deep into
the dark booth. She shoots Nickie Handy dead from
the waist up.

Two soft little *pfftt*s that never make it up over
the din. Heart shots. Quick-like, because she doesn't
want to hurt him.

Nickie lies down on the scarred wooden table like
a good little drunk. He goes right off to sleep.

Carrie's mind is racing as she elbows her way out
onto the avenue. Two very good reasons for the
murder.

First of all, poor Nickie was one of the few people
left who could still identify her and Damian. Secondly,
she'd liked Nickie too much to let him live like that.
To let him go where he was obviously going.

Slightly dizzy from the bar scene, she crosses the
Avenue Marceau in a sea of Renaults, Simcas, wolf
whistles.

Up some side street. Stacked heels clicking, white
butterfly stockings singing silk.

She takes off the floppy white Easter bonnet. Tosses
it over a slat fence into somebody's yard. She takes off

the uncomfortable high-heeled pumps and gets into black flats out of her shoulder bag.

At Avenue Montaigne, she meets Damian. The two of them embrace for a long moment. Then the pretty young couple walk arm in arm across the murky, slow-moving Seine.

Almost at once, they begin to prepare to be double-crossed.

The effect that we wanted most on San Dominica was helpless confusion. A feeling like darkness and light being turned on and off at our will. Things suddenly being dangerous that weren't supposed to be dangerous. . . . More important, there had to be no way to chart any of it. No known patterns.

The Rose Diary

Wylde's Falls, San Dominica

Between seven Sunday morning and the late afternoon, nothing happened on San Dominica that hadn't been happening for the previous thousand years or so. The over one hundred and fifty beaches were pearly white, striking and perfect; the royal-blue skies were clear and pure—a thousand-percent improvement on any metropolitan sky; the sunshine was uninterrupted.

And while nothing terrifying was happening, the Americans and Europeans still on the island had time to sit back and think about *what had happened*. Not least of all, the sixty-one members of the government Assembly had time to consider their unlucky alternatives for the future.

At four in the afternoon, Colonel Dassie Dred stands on the verge of worldwide fame.

Looking down from the second highest and most beautiful waterfall in the Caribbean—Wylde's Falls— he can see a barefoot black boy and a white couple

145

making the popular walking tour up the many-tiered water shoots.

The three people slosh through the most beautiful black fresh-water pools. They splash together in cascading ten- and twenty-foot-high falls, occasionally shout to one another over the crashing roar of the blue water, stop once for a misty camera shot.

When the young guide finally turns the rocky corner beneath his hiding place, Dred extends his hand through a clump of bushes. The small boy allows himself to be pulled up, leaving the white couple looking up at the leering face of the revolutionary. "Yo' go home now," Dred says to the boy. "Nemmine be lookin' back."

As he speaks, two of his men jump through banana leaves into the bubbly pool below. One man comes swinging a cane machete sideways like a baseball bat.

The long knife catches a screaming, thirtyish woman across the chest of her *Town & Country* summer blouse. The hard blow upends her in a clumsy three-point fall.

The second, stronger soldier brings his knife straight down overhand. The woman's blond, bankerish husband stands still for a moment, then he splits from the shoulders down, toppling over Wylde's Falls.

Meanwhile, down at the park's entry gates, a handful of tourists and lounging guides are watching the day's final climbers make their way down the tricky falls.

As they watch two couples and their guides climb down slowly, a body—a swimming woman, it looks like—shoots head first around a high curve in the swift water. The swimming woman disappears again; then topples over a smooth lip of black rock; then catches sideways up against a jutting boulder shooting bubbly white water high in the air.

A man split like broken scissors comes down next.

146

The body makes it around the jutting rock, bounces down several small falls, skims past the terror-stricken crowd at the gates, then disappears without a sound into the sea.

Colonel Dred has conducted his first official machete raid and, as it has been skillfully designed to be, it's the very best one so far.

Dred is ready.

Trelawney, San Dominica

SUNDAY EVENING

A greasy dish of sticky brown rice sits in front of him. Gray shredded goat. Some shellfish that isn't lobster, isn't crab or shrimp, isn't really edible.

Peter Macdonald thinks he sees a small black claw rise up and swim in the stew. He gobbles it anyway. It's sixty cents for the meal and green tea—a bargain.

After his Sunday dinner, Macdonald sits in a dark rear corner of the native restaurant. He slowly smokes two cigarettes. He nervously pushes his hand back through his hair twenty or thirty times within five minutes or less.

Sitting there all alone, Peter remembers a dumb movie he'd seen once. Some handsome blond actor had played a man who'd simply gone to the New York *Times* to get out of a pack of trouble. Gone to the *Times* the way people used to go to the police— and the next thing you knew, everything was copacetic. The man in the movie was safe and sound.

The screen credits rolled up over the man's frozen, smiling face. "America the Beautiful" played. Everybody in the theater went home happy as clams.

Idle speculations of a drowning man.

Because what exactly could *he* tell the New York *Times,* Peter had begun to speculate. What could he tell anybody, really?

That he'd seen this tall blond Englishman—maybe an Englishman—in the vicinity of *one* of the San Dominica machete murders? That he'd held a State Department man's face to the burner of an electric stove, and the man had begun to scream about the Mafia?

Suddenly, the restaurant's waitress/cook is standing over him.

A small, moon-faced black girl, she's been flitting around the main room like a trapped moth all night. *Table . . . table . . . window . . . window . . . stove . . . table . . . window.*

Nobody will let the moth-girl out, though . . . *table.*

"Yo' lak yo' lobster, yes, mahn?" Loose translation: *You're crazy to eat in here. Let me outside, please. I'm a moth.*

Peter smiles at the moth thought; at something in the young girl's eyes. "Good food," he says softly. "Better than at the big hotels."

The waitress remembers the words later for the San Dominica police. She says that the young American left the restaurant around nine. That he'd gotten on a motorcycle outside.

The police tell her that the American man has gone a little crazy on account of all the murders. They say they want him for questioning. Nothing serious.

Coastown, San Dominica

Almost simultaneous with the police interview in the Trelawney restaurant, four men in expensive raw-silk suits—Park Avenue bankers, from the look of them—sit down to dinner on a handsome screened-in porch on a big estate in Coastown proper.

The four are: San Dominica's prime minister, Joe Walthey; Great Western Air Transport's Brooks Campbell; the Forlenza Family's Isadore Goldman; and Goldman's man on San Dominica, a beachboy type named Duane Nicholson.

The meal that the four men are served begins with Chincoteagues; then a Montrachet; stuffed lamb *en ballon;* buttered celery; corn. In the wings is a grand Floating Island. All in all, a most delicious, civilized feast.

On and off, the men watch the leggy mistress of Prime Minister Walthey swimming laps in the blue-bottomed pool that stretches out directly in front of the porch.

On and off, Izzie Goldman tries to explain the facts of life and death to the other three.

A thin, liver-spotted hand floats out in front of the gangster as he speaks.

"I'm seventy-five years old," he says quietly, so that they all have to concentrate on his words. "I don't understand why you ask me all these schoolboy questions about the Roses." Goldman sighs. "Why can't you let them do their work? Pay the money and forget about it."

"Because they're a liability," Brooks Campbell says to him. "Because I have my orders from way, way up the ladder."

The old man takes a bird bite of his lamb.

"They're too smart to carry tales." He talks and chews. "I don't understand why everybody is trying so hard to make another Bay of Pigs catastrophe here."

"This is hardly the liberation of Cuba." Campbell points a finger at the old man. "And, besides, I think Rose has gone crazy. We never saw any plans like this. A few murders, yes. Massacres, no."

The prime minister of San Dominica brushes a fly away from his wine.

Joseph Walthey, "Joe," is a short, stocky black. Forty-one years old. A demagogue, and potentially a dictator. The black man has a neat pencil mustache, a big thumb of a nose, a very bumpy, pocked complexion.

"Just for the sake of . . . dinner talk"—he speaks with a soft, diplomatic lilt—"why won't you answer a few of our questions, Mr. Goldman? What possible harm could come from ridding the world of these two murderers, for example?"

The old man sinks even farther into his big rattan chair. His gray suit coat bunches terribly around a pink-and-brown silk tie. Pink flamingos are crushed all over the tie.

The prime minister's girl friend crashes into the

pool again and Izzie Goldman hears an insane old song start up in his mind.

Hubba hubba, ding ding
Baby, you got everything
What a face, what a figger!
What a shame that you're a nigger!

Vaude-ville—bring it back! Please! Quick!

"Above and beyond everything else that's wrong here"—he glances across the table at Brooks Campbell—"I don't think you'll catch them. Let them go back to France, Mr. Campbell, Prime Minister. Let it end after tomorrow. Trust me on this."

To his immediate left, Duane Nicholson sits flicking ashes from his cigarette into his empty dinner plate.

"No. We want the Roses dead," Brooks Campbell repeats. "That's our position."

Isadore Goldman stares at the beachboy Nicholson before making his next statement on the matter.

"The people who put their cigarettes in their plates," the old man finally says, "should have to eat out of their ashtrays."

And those are absolutely Isadore Goldman's last words on the fiasco.

Trelawney, San Dominica

A little after nine, Peter Macdonald hides the BMW motorcycle in thick brush, then walks inside the Trelawney bus station.

The station is one small, dim room that smells like an army has stopped to urinate and de-louse there.

Peter examines a schedule for buses going across the island to Port Gerry. At Port Gerry, he thinks he has a way to get off San Dominica safely. A way to get some help. *Maybe.* The question is whether to travel anonymously by bus, or quickly by bike.

None of the hangarounds inside the station seem to be noticing him, he believes. That's good, at least.

He sits down on one of the long gray benches. Sees a newspaper headline crumpled up under another seat. DOUBLE MURDERS! DRED ON MOVE.

Almost 9:15 now . . . Starting to miss Jane like hell. Remembering what it was like to be lonely.

He begins to read a six-foot-by-ten-foot-wide community blackboard. A child's handwriting, it looks like.

NOW THAT ELECTION RESULTS ALL OVER THE CARIB-BEAN HAVE TURNED OUT VICTORIOUS FOR SOCIALISTS,

AND JOE IS SERIOUSLY ILL, I THINK WE SHOULD TAKE A LONG LOOK AT COMING ELECTION.

JOE'S PLAYBOY ATTITUDE IS UNBECOMING AN EXECUTIVE TO OFFICE. PROFESSOR SAM HAS ONLY FOUR YEARS OF SCHOOLING (CHECK RECORDS OF THE BAINTY SCHOOL IN COASTOWN), WHILE I AM, AS YOU KNOW, GRADUATE OF THE UNIVERSITY OF THE WEST INDIES.

THOSE OF YOU WHO VOTE FOR "JOE" ARE VOTING FOR THE FOLLOWING: MORE CONTROL BY FOREIGNERS —CIA, HIGH PRICES, LOW WAGES, MORE CONTROL BY FOREIGNERS, WILDNESS IN STREETS BY COLONEL DRED, NO PRICE CONTROLS, UNSANITARY—WITH FOOD SPREAD ON THE GROUND WHERE WE WALK, SPIT, ETC., TO BE SOLD TO CONSUMERS. MORE CONTROL BY FOREIGNERS. EVEN DRED HIMSELF WOULD BE PREFERRED BETTER THAN OLD BLACK "JOE."

TOMMY (THOMAS WYASS)

Macdonald the Sign Reader. Looking for direction? Clues? *More control by foreigners. Prime Minister Joe Walthey. Dred on move.*

Peter reads: FORBIDDEN IN THIS TERMINAL: SMOKING, SCREAMING, OBSCENE LANGUAGE, SHELLING OF PEANUTS, EATING OF CHEWING GUM. THANK YOU. TOMMY.

Peter is chewing gum, smoking, screaming obscene language inside his brain.

He goes into a dark, wooden phone booth where he can chew and smoke his brains out in peace.

He thinks about where he ought to spend the night. Port Gerry? The woods again? . . . No one ever teaches you how to survive in America. Not even the Army, really. They just teach the Army how to survive.

Finally, against all his previous resolves, against his whole idea of trying to keep her out of this, Peter decides that he has to call Jane.

First he calls her friends in Coastown.

She's left, they tell him. Jane has gone back to the inn. *Shit. Shit. Shit. Shit.*

Peter makes the call to Turtle Bay. Number ninety. The Plantation Inn.

Switchboard operator.

"Cottage Number Fourteen, please . . .

"Janie, it's me. Peter. I've been trying to call you all day in Coastown."

"Oh, Peter! Where are you?"

There's a short pause on his end of the line.

"I want you to go back to the States," Peter finally says. "See what Westerhuis can do to get you on a flight out of here . . . Janie?"

"Dammit all to hell, Macdonald! Tell me where you are. Cool it, Peter."

Peter smiles for a second. *That's Jane.* He stops the melodramatics and tells her where he's been for the past day. Then he tells her what he thinks they ought to do now. What they shouldn't do.

Only after he's gone through it all—the talk about himself—does Jane mention the Blond Englishman.

"He was here, Peter."

Small, shocking statement. *He was here.*

"I saw him this afternoon. I think . . . It had to be him. He was blond, maybe six foot two. . . ."

Peter stops her. Suddenly, it's as if he's a combat officer again. Giving orders that must be followed.

"I want you to lock and latch all the doors and windows right now, Jane."

"Everything is locked. Just come and get me."

He tries to visualize the room. The cottage itself. Fool's Hot Toast. He tries to imagine how he would go about attacking it. Defending it.

"All right, that's good. Will you turn off all the lights in there? Do it right now, okay?"

"Okay! Okay!"

He hears the sound of the phone being set down.

He's been right there. Peter considers again. *Come down into the inn as if he has some kind of diplomatic immunity. Brass balls, at least.*

Suddenly, he has a quick flash of the tall blond figure standing over Turtle Bay four days earlier. Looking as if he owned the place. Looking as if he owned the goddamn world.

Then Jane is back on the phone. Whispering, all of a sudden.

"It's pitch black in here," she tells him. "I can see a couple walking out on the beach. Oh, Peter, this is so creepy I don't believe it's happening."

"For what it's worth," Peter says, "I'm on my way."

Turtle Bay, San Dominica

The sound outside Cottage Number 14 is something like *bomp*.

Bomp, bomp . . . bomp, bomp, bomp.

The noise stops suddenly, and Jane Cooke stands perfectly still, quiet and afraid, inside the dark bedroom.

First she catches her breath, then she tries to figure the sound out.

Rose apples—she finally solves the small mystery. The noise is rose apples dropping onto the bungalow roof.

Jane realizes that she's letting herself get a little confused now. *Stop it. Grab control.*

One of her hands slides along the cool limestone wall. Her cheek goes against the wall. Long blonde hair presses against it.

Her fingers grope along the sloppily laid wallpaper. Ruffles. Air pockets. Then an end to the wall altogether . . . doorjamb . . . gritty bathroom tile.

She puts her face under the faucet. Soaks herself. Drinks some rusty-tasting water.

Then Jane puts the toilet seat cover down and sits.

Takes cigarettes out of her T-shirt pocket. Looks down and sees the dark outline of a book on the floor. *All the President's Men.* Their bathroom book.

She smokes three cigarettes while thinking about her and Peter's situation. She hears another small noise. . . . Bettles flying against the windows. *Woof!* Like getting punched in the stomach. . . . Then she figures she ought to be out where she can at least watch the front window.

The big window at the front of the bungalow is showing a crystal-clear black-and-white movie.

No more couple walking on the beach . . . Thin, smoky, purplish clouds drifting past a full moon. Old, shriveled night clouds. A low line of frothy white surf running around the cove, outlining it like whipped cream.

She'd been all right until Peter had called, Jane starts to think. . . .

A lot of men had ogled her around the inn. Even tall blond ones. Even tall blond ones who *might* look a little English . . .

Nice girl from the capital city of South Dakota, she thinks. . . . Boyfriend accidentally witnesses a murder. Just a glance. No more than ten seconds! Must be an Alfred Hitchcock film. . . . Macabre throughout, ghoulish like *Frenzy,* but a happy ending. Ingrid Bergman and Cary Grant clink champagne glasses, then kiss.

Thinking about the tall blond Englishman again. *The Tall Blond Englishman.* Can't keep her hands from shaking now. Funny—*odd,* that is.

He'd been drinking by himself on the Pineapple Terrace. A very good-looking, serious man. Nice tan. Black wraparound glasses that made her think of the Mediterranean.

She thought he'd been watching her while she taught

a little girl how to get water out of her ear. *"First, hop on the foot opposite the clogged-up ear. Here—like this, silly-face. Now. Bang the side of your head. Bang it good. . . ."*

After that, she was sure the blond man was following her. Keeping her in sight, anyway. Well, he *seemed* to be. . . .

Jane looks down at her watch. Glowing red numbers in the dark bedroom: 10:43.

An hour and ten minutes has passed since Peter called. . . . Usually the ride from Coastown took just over an hour. Add five minutes more from Trelawney.

Standing there beside the dark front window, she hears another onslaught of apples on the roof. *More blasted rose apples.*

Then footsteps.

Then a young woman is outside, calling her name at the front door. . . .

And then one of the shuttered windows is being broken down with something sharp and powerful like an ax.

MASSACRE AT ELIZABETH'S FANCY

The planning is usually interesting. Getting close to the final time is interesting. But the climax, the big kill, is usually something of an *anti*climax. . . . Not to the victims, of course.

The Rose Diary

May 5, 1975; Mandeville, San Dominica

MONDAY MORNING, THE SEVENTH DAY OF THE SEASON

At 4:00 A.M. on the seventh day, Jane's eyes pop open wide.

She sees nothing at first. Then the long shadow of a man sitting by her bed. Then bright afterimages of running men and machetes. And a tall woman who speaks very sweetly, as if she's Jane's best friend.

As she begins to scream, a night lamp clicks on. A shiny aluminum lamp nailed to the wall.

The man sitting underneath the light is the chief of police. He has a small black pipe stuck in his mouth. A holster and gun are slung over his short-sleeved white shirt.

"*Shhhhhh* . . . You're in the Mandeville Hospital," he whispers to the blonde girl. "You're all right. Everything is all right now."

The black man smiles and winks at her, then he clicks the light off.

Jane lies in the dark shivering badly. Her teeth begin to click together and she starts to cry. Thinking about Peter. Just wanting to hold tight. Hold tight.

"What is happening?"

She isn't sure whether she's *said* the words out loud, or just *thought* them loud. She starts to shiver; then to cry; then to hug herself because it's so damn awful.

Then she's sleeping again.

In her dreams, they come to the hospital for her. They come somewhere for her.

The two black men. The tall blond man with the wraparound sunglasses. The young woman . . . They keep screaming at her to tell them where Peter is. . . .
"I don't know! I don't know! Please don't hurt me."

The wall lamp clicks back on again.

The heavyset, black police chief smiles at her. He puts his forefinger to his lips. Makes a little fire in the bowl of his black pipe.

"Shhhh. Shhhh. No one can hurt you now," Dr. Johnson says.

Even though the worst day of the Season of the Machete has begun.

Cape John, San Dominica

MONDAY AFTERNOON

Like a white kite in the wind, a sea gull swings back and forth high over his head.

Aaaaa! Aaaaa! Aaaaa!

Lying in a buttery midday sun, Damian feels a wonderful calm begin to drift over him. He and Carrie are approaching a definite bench mark now. The last of the island's Terrors.

Ah—there is nothing like being in the sun for reviving one's prospects.

He can feel the salt water drying on his face and legs. The hot sun broiling him in a way that makes it seem rather fun.

For perhaps the five hundredth time, Damian reviews the final details in his mind. The massacree. Carrie's, then his own, escape.

There will be no Nickie Handy–style double crosses this time out. No meeting up with Brooks Campbell or Harold Hill in dark, deserted alleyways.

All that's left for him now is to set out a last, tasty morsel of bait for Great Western Air Transport. Something for King Rat Brooks Campbell to nibble on.

Then a check on the plot's final playing piece—a tricky, strong-arm killer named Clive Lawson.

Then it's home again, home again, jiggity jog.

Mandeville, San Dominica

At 1:00 P.M., a man in a summer sports coat and white hat takes a deep breath, then approaches an old woman in a Red Cross hat, who sits at the first floor reception desk inside Mandeville Hospital.

"My name is Max Westerhuis," the man announces in an impatient, self-important tone. "I'm told I have to come to this desk to get a pass to see Miss Cooke."

The elderly nurse reaches into her desk drawer. She takes out a plain brown clipboard. She checks a list of visitors cleared to see hospital patients that is written on sheets of paper attached to the board.

There is only one visitor cleared for Miss J. Cooke in Room 206.

The nurse writes out a slip for *Maximilian Westerhuis, manager of the Plantation Inn.*

As the policeman posted at Room 206 opens the door for him, the man in the white hat puts a finger to his lips.

"Miss Cooke," he says, in the same official tone he'd used at the front desk.

"Peter," Jane whispers as soon as he's closed the door behind him.

She looks very pale and shaken to him. Large gauze bandages are wrapped around her neck and both arms; an intravenous bottle hangs over the bed.

Peter goes to her and they hold one another tightly, saying things that should have been said long before then; expressing feelings they'd both been afraid of.

As they finally pull apart, Jane begins to tell him about the three people who'd come to their cottage at the Plantation Inn. How they'd wanted to know where he was hiding. All the things they'd done to try and make her talk . . . For his part, Peter tells Jane about his surprise visit at Brooks Campbell's; the Mafia connection; the big blowup that's apparently coming soon.

"Well, what do we do now?"

"The first thing—I want to get you out of this hospital. We must be dealing with a black version of the Keystone Kops here. Look at how easily I got in."

"Peter, if they'd been after me—*they had me* last night. All they wanted to know was where *you* were."

"That doesn't make complete sense. If you did see him yesterday, they'd want you too. Wouldn't they? Oh, hell, I don't know what's going on around here."

The twenty-four-year-old man sits down on the hospital bed. His shoulders begin to sag. His neck muscles feel unbelievably tense and twisted.

"Peter, did you see anything that day *besides* the blond man?"

"I don't know. I don't think I did. . . .

"The best solution I can come up with," Peter finally says, "is that we both have to get off San Dominica. I want to try Washington." He looks at Jane. "Will you meet me there? In a day—a few days. There's a hotel in Washington called the Hay-Adams. It's right across from the White House."

For the first time that afternoon, Jane smiles. "Good. Then we can take this thing right to the top. We can't do any worse than at the U.S. Embassy, right?" She kisses him hard, then rests her head on his shoulder. "Darling Max."

"Somebody's going to listen to us. It can't be this unbelievably fucked-up everywhere."

Jane smiles again. "Maximilian Westerhuis! God, Peter."

They both start to laugh, hushing one another so the guard doesn't come in. Then they hug again, secure their pact to meet in Washington by Wednesday, and Peter goes out of the hospital the very same way he'd originally come in.

Much, much too easily.

Coastown, San Dominica

Inside the Princess Hotel meanwhile, Carrie sits with the gleaming white doors to her loggia flung open wide.

Bright sunshine and a sympathetic breeze drift in. Smells of fresh flowers come up from a pretty glen two stories below.

Carrie stares hard at the garish face looking back at her from the dressing-room mirror.

She's marginally, begrudgingly satisfied that her face looks about right for what it has to do.

A subtle touch of razzle-dazzle. Real-hair half-lashes. Close attention to detail, right down to her silver slippers.

Carrie checks her wristwatch. If everything goes well, she's about six hours away from Washington now. All she has to do is slip quietly past the police, the CIA, and half the Army of San Dominica.

At 1:30 on the dot, Carrie Rose leaves for Robert Kennedy Airport with her fingers, legs, and eyes crossed. And when she walks into the airport terminal, Carrie discovers that her dressing-room preparation has really been quite thorough. She needn't have worried.

She looks like just about every other woman there.

By 2:30, Carrie Rose is on a Pan Am flight out of the Caribbean.

When the three o'clock news from Puerto Rico comes on the brassy transistor radio nearby, Damian starts to gather up his clothes.

The tall blond man puts on dark sunglasses, a white deck-hand's hat, a plain white cotton-madras shirt.

At 3:10, he walks into a shabby open-air café. The outdoor restaurant runs the length of Cape John Beach on thin, crusty gray pilings—pelican's legs.

From a café pay phone, Rose calls the American Embassy.

Receptionist.

Male secretary.

Put on hold.

Three-seventeen.

Three-twenty-one. Getting slightly humorous.

Brooks Campbell finally speaks. "Hello, this is Campbell."

Damian says, "Listen very carefully and don't say a fucking word until I'm finished. . . . In fifty-four minutes, at four-fifteen, Colonel Dred is going to commit his first major act of violence. This will be the *final* act we've planned for you. . . ."

"Rose! . . ."

"Shut the fuck up! . . . We expect you to try and stop us from leaving San Dominica after this. But if you do, I'm going to kill you. I promise you, Campbell. Here's to poor Nickie Handy, chump."

"Rose."

CLICK.

"Goddammit, stop playing games!" Brooks Campbell screams into the loud buzzing of the telephone.

Shortly after Rose's call, Campbell contacts Harold Hill in Washington.

"All hell is about to break loose here. I'm going to need a lot of help now. But I'm going to get them, Harry."

"I think you will. I really do," says Harry the Hack. *CLICK.*

At 5:30, feeling desperate and confused, Peter Macdonald telephones Campbell at the U.S. Embassy.

He's informed by a very official-sounding American man that Mr. Campbell has left for the day. Peter is then told that all Americans are being asked to stay off the streets.

There's been a massacre. *CLICK.*

Elizabeth's Fancy, San Dominica

Tyndall's Goat Highway goes nowhere except a restored nineteenth-century sugar-cane plantation called Elizabeth's Fancy—and when Elizabeth's Fancy closes at four each afternoon, the Goat Highway goes nowhere.

The last bus from the plantation carries the final tour groups back to their hotels. It also brings back a woman ticket-taker, a forty-two-year-old bartender-manager from Liverpool, England, and three security guards from Tanner Men.

The bus is a tongue-red–and–black double-decker manufactured by Rolls-Royce in 1953. Its nickname is "Grasshopper."

Grasshopper has a maximum speed of forty-four mph, and misaligned springs that make it appear to hop down the bumpy Goat Highway.

Because its second deck rides so much higher than the jungle brush, Grasshopper can be seen literally from five miles away.

In this case, however, the red top half of the bus is being observed from just two miles off.

The three black men standing at the edge of the Goat Highway all hold high-powered M-16 rifles manufactured in Detroit, Michigan. Just behind them stands a line of teen-age boys. Each boy holds a sharp machete knife.

"How'd you compare dis M-sixteen an' th' old M-fourteen?" Colonel Dred is saying to the African.

Kingfish Toone's eyes don't move away from the dirt road. Right beside him, the Cuban is toeing dust like a stubborn or angry horse. He is looking forward to shooting Dred very much now.

"There is no comparison." The African's deep voice finally comes. "The M-sixteen will strike any target with three times the impact of a conventional rifle. It would shoot straight through a line of five men." The mercenary takes a silver bullet out of his shirt pocket. He holds the bullet lengthwise between thick, coal-black fingers.

"Still another war toy. Invented by the Americans, I suppose. The shell is coated with plastic. It leaves no stains. Impossible to find with a medical X-ray. Quite diabolical, really. Think about it, Colonel Dred."

"Dey cost?" the guerrilla asks. "Th' guns, nah dose bullet. Diabolik bullet you have."

"I don't follow costs very closely." Toone shrugs. "Perhaps five hundred apiece for the rifles."

"*Hyiuuu.*" The guerrilla chief shrieks and laughs. Then Dred walks away to make a last check on his soldiers.

In the back of his mind is the delicious thought that within hours he will be more important than Che, maybe even than Fidel Castro. Something like a black Arafat . . . Holding the sun for ransom instead of oil.

The driver of the red bus, forty-nine-year-old Franklin James, is feeling sweaty and itchy, and most of all malcontent, this particularly sweaty afternoon.

As the antique double-decker bumps along, he can feel the whole Goat Highway in the palm of his hand. In the shivering black knob of the stick shift.

Jus' what is th' problem now? James talks to himself. *Tired of drivin' dis funny-time bus. Earnin' yo' money too easy, hey mon? Want to break yo' ass for it lak nigger? Admit it, mon, yo' got it easy. Admit to yo'self, truth, Franklin. . . .*

Just to break the everyday monotony, though, the driver thinks he'll do something revolutionary today: go left instead of right at the V in the road about a quarter of a mile ahead.

He'll take the scenic route instead of the Goat Highway this day. Through the old sugar-cane fields.

Franklin James looks back in his mirror and sees straw beach hats and lobster-red faces. A pretty blonde bitch in a halter top is playing with her tittie straps. There are a few empty seats for a change, too.

At the V in the road, the bus driver takes a left instead of the usual Goat Highway route.

As he makes the wrong turn, the red-faced manager of Elizabeth's Fancy jumps up in the third seat of the bus.

"This is the wrong road, you idiot bastard. Back it up, boy. Get back on the goat road."

Which Franklin James does with a subservient smile, and not a word of protest. *Admit it, mon, yo' got it easy.*

Most of Dred's men are lying on their stomachs back twenty to forty yards from the dirt road.

A few bare-chested boys have shimmied up into coconut trees.

Colonel Dred is paying no attention. Instead, the twenty-seven-year-old man watches the burly African and the Cuban.

A man smoking a cigarette and wearing a striped woolen hat shouts to Dred from out of a tree.

"Dey comin' 'round in 'bout anudder minute."

The soldier flips his cigarette butt down out of the tree.

Monkey Dred turns and gives a silent hand gesture to the rest of his guerrillas. The sounds of rifles clicking echoes on both sides of the Goat Highway.

Then Dred puts the sleek M-16 to his own cheek. He sights it very carefully.

Squeezes.

Squeezes.

The whole top half of the Cuban's head splatters. Blood splashes onto tall stalks of grass as far as thirty feet away. Kingfish Toone is thrown forward with his huge black arms stretched out wide, a big dark hole in the back of his khaki shirt.

"Bad kind a niggers," Monkey Dred shouts to the soldier in the tree. "Drivin' Cadillac. Warin' parfuume, yo' know."

Besides, the executions have been well paid for by Damian Rose. They've earned Dred two more precious machine guns.

Speckles of red splash through a latticework of jungle green. Then Colonel Dred can see the upper deck of the bus again.

Sun rays ricochet off the scaling red roof. Some banana wrens pass by. Every window in the old bus is flung open wide.

Americans, Germans, English, South Americans look out on handsome mahogany trees, blooming wild lilies, parakeets without cages.

Jungle, mahn, jungle.

"Ay pretty!" Dred shouts to the treetop birds. Jacamars. Parrots.

His adrenaline is flowing like the teeming streets of Trenchtown. The juices make him feel like a Rastafarian superman. *Jah*. A walking, fast-talking contradiction.

The teetering double-decker bus has turned down a narrow straightaway less than a hundred yards away.

It's coming straight at them, down a tunnel of coconut and fir trees.

Dred's men begin to talk to one another. Enthusiastic shouts. Hypertense babble.

The red bus is fuzzy and just a little unreal through
shimmering heat waves. High blond weeds fan away
from it like flying hair. Palms and ferns loudly scrape
the roof and windows.

Dred is staring so hard, anticipating so very much,
that the bus seems to stop moving. To freeze on the
straightaway.

"Ro-bert!" he screams. "Ro-bert!"

A tiny rifleman with sick yellow eyes and a yellow
Che beret comes running up beside him. The man's
big M-16 rifle makes him seem a child.

"Stay by me, Robert. Now watch closely. I want
you to shoot it."

As if the red bus is a charging elephant.

Up ahead, Franklin James watches a young woman and small boy step into the Goat Highway. Barefooted, dressed in sun-bleached rags, they stand in the middle of the road, both of them waving excitedly at the bus.

James curses to himself, but he touches his foot to the brakes.

He shifts gears, and before the bus fully stops, has the folding doors crashing open.

"Hey, what is it, woman?" the fat black man shouts angrily.

"Yo' can take us to main road?" the woman screams through the open bus door. "Bway is bahd sick, mon."

The bus driver's face takes on a pained look. "Oh, lay-dy! I can't ride no-body not fram dat plantation, yo' know."

"My bway is sick!" the black woman screams.

Suddenly, a rifle shot crashes through the top right corner of the bus windshield. The entire right half of the windshield falls back inside the bus.

Franklin James puts his foot to the ground and the Grasshopper bucks and jumps forward.

The hollow, popping sound of M-16 rifles erupts everywhere.

Not thirty yards away from Dred's men, the tall, gawky bus seems to strike a giant pothole.

The bus slides quietly to the center of the road. It seems to ride on its right tires for a while. Then the bus swerves sharply to the left.

Franklin James is already dead, bumping back and forth over the steering wheel. People inside the bus are falling out of their seats.

Like an enormous lawn mower, the double-decker runs over five- and six-foot-high ferns, thick brush, small trees. It hits a huge royal palm straight on, and the palm tree tears back through the engine and cab.

The tree trunk continues five feet down the aisle, crushing people in the front seats, and then the Grasshopper stops for good.

Gaping holes begin to mottle the side of the bus that faces into the firing squad.

On the second level of the bus, the Tanner security guards answer the rifle fire with a few pistol shots. When the guards are lucky, they manage to hit somewhere in the trees where Dred's men are systematically destroying the bus. Shooting it to bits.

The heads of dead passengers sit still in several of the open windows. The broken engine has begun to spew thick black smoke.

A few of the bus passengers climb out far-side windows, try to run, and are shot down.

A small blond boy in red shorts lies limp and dead in the grass to one side of the bus. An older man lies beside a big, black front tire.

A twelve-year-old girl runs like the horses on her father's farm—a beautiful little girl from Surrey, England—and she's a survivor.

For ten minutes, there is shouting and stomach-freezing screams from the forty-odd people trapped in the bus. Then there's no sound except for the lazy popping of M-16 rifles.

Colonel Dred and his marksman Robert walk to the bus in smoky, devastating silence. As they get up close, parrots and jacamars begin to scream in the trees again. The tiny marksman takes out a dull black Liberator pistol.

The two disappear into the bus and more gunshots are fired. A man screams inside the bus. Another muffled gunshot sounds inside.

When they come out again, Dred waves to the four boys standing up on the Goat Highway. Each of the four has a long, scary fright wig. Each holds a shiny field machete with a red neckerchief tied around the hilt.

At the same time, the other rebel soldiers are getting up out of the brush, dropping down from trees. The guerrillas begin to light up *ganja* sticks, regular cigarettes, cheap cigars. Only a few of them come forward to examine the bus.

It's Dred himself who sees the beige-and-green shadow moving through the thick backwoods behind the red bus.

He recognizes the face of Damian Rose, a pink smudge among the trees and bright green bushes. A shiny white smile.

"Aaagghh, Rose. Jeezus, mahn!"

The young guerrilla screams as he realizes what's going to happen. He tries to turn away.

The first rifle shot pierces the back of his head; it comes out where the black man's nose and mouth have been.

The wound is very hot, and for a split second Dred's

eyes and nose seem to be on fire. The ground rushes up at his face, and then it all disappears on him.

He's falling down a pitch-black hole that echoes his scream—*R . . . o . . . s . . . e . . . .*

By 6:00 P.M. *that night, the President of the United States knew about it.*

Five members of the Cabinet Committee to Combat Terrorism—the chief of staff; the assistant to the President for national security affairs; the press secretary for the President; the secretary of defense; and the director of the CIA—sat with him in the Oval Office of the White House.

The director of the CIA briefed the Chief Executive on selected facts about Lathrop Wells, Nevada; the Forlenzas; Isadore Goldman; Damian and Carrie Rose; San Dominica. His primary recommendation at the moment was that the contract operators Damian and Carrie Rose be eliminated immediately. Searched out and destroyed.

"You're shitting me," the President of the United States said after he'd heard the entire story.

The President looked around his Oval Office. At the chief of staff. At his press secretary. At his assistant for national security.

"Somebody tell me this man is shitting me. That's an order."

From 6:30 in the evening on, the world's TV and radio stations interrupted their regular programming to announce that the leftist San Dominican rebel, Colonel Dassie Dred, had been killed during an attack on a tourist bus some twenty-five miles east of the capital city of Coastown.

At 8:00 P.M., Carrie arrived in Washington, D.C. Now the tricky stuff began.

Part II

The Perfect Escape

BAY OF PIGS II

Damian and I had violent arguments about the Escape. My point of view: get out of the Caribbean immediately. Damian's: finish the operation as it should be finished. Take care of Campbell and Harold Hill right. Stop them from coming after us. . . . That was how Macdonald became important. Also how Damian got the idea for what happened in Washington.

The Rose Diary

May 6, 1975; Fairfax Station, Virginia

TUESDAY MORNING, THE EIGHTH DAY OF THE SEASON

The morning after the massacre at Elizabeth's Fancy, Mark Hill takes a fast shower; combs his thick blond hair; then puts on a freshly boraxed Washington Redskins sweatshirt and neat bell-bottom jeans.

The handsome teen-ager looks in the mirror over his bureau and gives himself an "okay" sign and a broad, comical wink.

Downstairs, he can hear his mother busily making breakfast.

Fried-bacon smells are drifting upstairs. Bacon, and

also fresh coffee, which Mark hates with a sincere passion.

The fourteen-year-old quickly brushes his teeth and uses the family Water Pik.

Then he takes the front stairs in three broad jumps. He strides casually into the kitchen, unconsciously imitating a pro football quarterback named Bill Kilmer.

Bright sunshine is streaming through the open back door and a saffron-curtained window over the sink.

A man and a woman in white terrorist masks stand in front of the sink, on either side of his mother. Each of the two holds a long-barreled black pistol.

"You just listen to what these people say." Carole Hill speaks in a calm voice that makes the boy wonder how his mother has gotten so brave so quickly.

Carrie Rose watches the boy through narrow eye slits in her mask.

"That's right, Mark. We're not here to hurt either of you. Sit down there at the table. Your mother will make you some breakfast."

Never once taking his eyes off the intruders, the teenager slowly sits down.

Carole Hill walks over to her stove slowly and cautiously. Her hands trembling, she starts to turn her bacon with a table fork. Little spits of grease fly up at her apron and face.

"My husband will be home soon," she says matter-of-factly. "He just—"

Carrie smiles under her mask. "Carole Ann, your husband isn't even in the country right now. Relax. Cook us all a nice breakfast, okay? We're going to be spending the day together, it looks like."

The man with her, a New York gunman by the name of Kruger, sits down across from Mark at the breakfast table.

The man reaches inside his raincoat. He takes out a

leather-sheafed field machete that he sets on the Hills' kitchen table.

"Pay it no mind," the man says. "Doesn't concern you, Mark."

"How do you know my name?" is the boy's first question.

"Oh, we're friends of your father's." Carrie smiles.

One girl's candid evaluation of the CIA's Caribbean Account in '75 . . . Basic ineptitude down to a formal science. An inordinate paranoia about Fidel Castro, and/or Moscow. Paranoia about potential trouble in Puerto Rico. Paranoia over Cuban troops in Africa. A gross overestimation of Dassie Dred. A correct evaluation of Joseph Walthey as a potential strong-arm pig and ally. . . . Mostly bad information of all things. Bad Intelligence . . .

The Rose Diary

Coastown, San Dominica

That same morning in Coastown, forty-four-year-old Harold Hill yawns so that his jaw cracks.

He stretches his thin arms, and makes eating noises with his lips, teeth, sticky furred tongue. He takes his horn-rimmed glasses off and massages the bridge of his nose.

Harold Hill then rearranges himself in a sighing, wingback chair inside the U.S. Embassy.

He glances through an Army report on Peter Macdonald: *Peter Stillwell Macdonald. Born Grand Rapids, Michigan; 1950. Son of a U.S. Army colonel and a high-school mathematics teacher. Youngest of six sons. U.S.M.A. 1969–71. Dropped out for personal reasons . . . Above-average intelligence. Inferiority complex caused in part by older brothers' successes . . . Mixes well but prefers to stay alone . . . No close friends . . . Subject of homosexual probe ('73—all branches): negative . . . Strong combat skills but ambivalent attitude about current war. A model top sergeant . . .*

Tossing aside that report, Hill looks back at a yellow legal pad where he's been free-associating about the Roses. He looks at a black folder marked "Secret— Sensitive." Then back at the legal pad.

It's 5:00 A.M., and Hill hasn't slept since six the previous morning.

At the top of the yellow, blue-lined sheet, "Carrie & Damian Rose" is centered and underlined in red. The rest of the paper is covered with neat black handwriting in orderly columns. Ideas, phrases, names, reminders . . . Fourteen items.

1. *Tall. Blond. English-looking. Has shopped at Harrods.*

2. *St. Louis Hotel in Paris . . . Nickie Handy shot by woman in nearby bistro. Carrie? . . . Handy used by Campbell (1972). Coincidence?*

3. *Carrie: fair-haired; supposed to be a stunner; tall . . . Beware! Don't be a chauvinist, shithead! Carrie is as dangerous as Damian.*

4. *Husband and wife squabbles . . . Absolutely . . . So what?*

5. *Dr. Meral Johnson. Street-smarts. Useful? How best?*

6. *Peter Macdonald should be found today. Cajoled. Useful!!!!*

7. *Marines from South America. Colonel Fescoe. Hindrance!!*

8. *Prop planes going out at night. Marijuana to New Orleans. Shoot down? Shoot down.*

9. *Coast Guard can blockade island effectively. . . . Search private craft especially . . . Would Goldman help Roses escape? Think so . . .*

10. *Can't let Joseph Walthey go crazy executing Dred's people. This is important.* *****

11. *Why Damian Rose phone calls to Campbell? Important!*

12. *Clue in their organized disorganization also. Important! . . . Stu Leedman coming from L.A. . . . Czech: killing team on Rose's level on loan from Interpol. Hindrance!!*

13. *Lucky 13! Damian probably a psycho.*

14. *Pattern suggests bigger plays to come. Antipattern suggests no further plays. . . . Operative word is "play." Have to learn to "play," or lose this one in grand style.*********

Harold Hill gets up and paces around the large oak-and-brass Embassy office. VIP office: like the presidential suite at famous hotels. Private bath, breakfast nook. The nuts!

There is no way the Roses are going to get off San Dominica, he considers.

No, there's a way, plenty of ways—but Hill is trying to convince himself that Damian Rose has programmed himself to make a mistake before he takes one of them. . . . The telephone calls to Brooks Campbell. Those are the key. Crank calls!

Harold Hill doesn't have very much to go on—but he does have something: Damian Rose is a tall, blond, English-looking *megalomaniac.* With luck, he can be had.

Hill finally puts his cream suit jacket over his arm and walks out of the big, cool Embassy mansion.

He believes that he's made a beginning at least. A good night's work.

A big red sun is just coming over the green hills that rise high over the perfect little city and the sea. It's a loud sun that will eventually give Hill a headache that day.

Two badly trained soldiers stand out by the front gates laughing and poking at one another. They remind Hill how little the people of these countries ever get involved in the realities of their situation.

As he passes by the soldiers, Hill tips his Panama hat and smiles. As he does so, he automatically thinks of the famous poster mocking Richard Nixon. *Why is this man smiling?* the poster says. Why, indeed?

If everything went as Damian expected it to, we were to meet at the Hilton Hotel in Morocco on or around May 10. If not, not.

The Rose Diary

Cap Foyle, San Dominica

At a quarter past five on May 6, Peter has an old James Taylor song blasting in his head—"Sweet Baby James." He is also being mesmerized by the sight of twenty black soldiers guarding the remains of the bus from Elizabeth's Fancy.

The young American watches the quiet, terrible scene for ten or fifteen minutes, plants it forever in his war-atrocities file, then leaves to forage around for something to eat.

For some disconnected reason, he has the Super Six on his mind: Neddy, Huey, Deli Bob, Bernie, Tailspin Tommy. And little Pete—Little Mac. As he rides away from the ambushed bus, Peter can't help thinking that *in his humble opinion*, he is way, way out of his league right now. Even in Special Forces they didn't prepare you for this kind of miserable shit.

At about that same time, Damian Rose pinches a blue mite off the sleeve of a pale-sand overshirt.

At 5:30 A.M., he stands tall and wide awake inside a phone booth in the neolithic farming village of Cap Foyle.

Rose asks for Number 26, and waits for his connection.

Two sleepy Cap Foyle residents, an old man and a girl, are already pushing skeletal bicycles along the town's dusty streets. Two cross streets down from them is the sharp green Caribbean.

"Hello . . . I said hello—"

Damian cuts off Brooks Campbell by shouting at the sleepy-sounding man—*screaming* at the top of his lungs into the telephone.

"You only have eight hours, asshole! Eight hours to decide to stop chasing us. To live up to your side of our contract. . . . If you're looking for us by midnight tonight, I guarantee both you and Hill will be sorrier than you can dream. I guarantee it! You have until midnight to be intelligent for once in your pitiful little grease-stain lives."

Damian then hangs up the phone. The tall blond man walks back to his car humming a favorite tune— "Lili Marlene." He's beginning to enjoy his escape plan.

Meanwhile, twelve rather striking-looking men are making their separate ways to San Dominica.

They're coming from Miami and New York. From Acapulco, Caracas, San Juan.

Each of the twelve is an expensive male model. From the Ford Agency. From Wilhelmina Men. From Stewart and Zoli.

They'd all been hired by Carrie the week before. To pose for brochures for the new Le Pirat Hotel, and for Dragon Reef Condominium Homes. They'd been specially selected off composite and head sheets at rates of $500 plus expenses per day.

The peculiar thing is that all twelve men are between six foot two and six foot four.

All are strikingly blond.

All look terribly, terribly English.

Part two of the curious adventure has begun. The perfect escape.

Casinos are now being built by all the big hotels.
. . . The island will have one bad season. Maybe
two. Maybe even three. But then it will boom like
nothing even they can imagine. The island has
four times the area of Nassau and New Provi-
dence. It's twice as beautiful as Jamaica. It should
become Monte-Carlo West.

The Rose Diary

"These days, it is fashionable to be against the
Americans. It is my hope to be in the vanguard of
a countermovement, which, I suspect, could be
equally fashionable one day. That is—to be for the
Americans."

Joseph Walthey

Coastown, San Dominica

TUESDAY AFTERNOON

While all this is going on, Brooks Campbell sits
hunched over a steaming pot of very strong, very good
Blue Mountain coffee from Jamaica. During the morning and early afternoon of May sixth, the young CIA
man makes person-to-person, heart-to-heart telephone
calls to some of the best homicide men in the world.

In the big office next door, Harold Hill is doing much the same thing on a slightly larger scale.

Calls go out to Mr. Alexander Somerset, the commissioner of crime at Scotland Yard; to Edward Mahoney in the Office of Domestic Intelligence in Washington; to the Assassination Bureau in Paris. Calls go to the biggest crime men in West Germany, Italy, Spain, Canada. . . .

The subject is top priority and very confidential, the conversations make clear.

A very large, very private manhunt is now being conducted throughout the Caribbean and South America. The objects of the hunt are two slithery, white soldiers of fortune who have taught a ragtag band of guerrillas how to fight and think like Mau-Maus, the PLO, and the Japanese Army. Who have, among other things, massacred a bus with forty-nine civilians on board. The names are Damian and Carrie Rose.

The slip-catch is that the United States is handling the search like a top-secret, national security matter. The clear implication: somebody has goofed again in the Caribbean.

The exact nature of the mistake remains a secret. A top secret.

Before it's over, though, some wisenheimer at Interpol has nicknamed the operation Bay of Pigs II. By Sunday, that slogan is a headline in London's *Observer.*

Beginning *unofficially* at 6:00 P.M. on May 5, *officially* at 9:00 A.M. on the sixth, a straight-faced, very serious attempt is made to take the eighty-one-by-thirty-nine-mile island of San Dominica, *turn it upside down,* and shake, shake, shake it like a child's piggy bank.

The long-shot hope is that both Roses and Peter Macdonald will tumble out into the waiting arms of Brooks Campbell and Harold Hill.

Beginning at nine, government sound trucks begin to rumble through major cities and the surrounding countryside.

These trucks broadcast the politest lilting-voiced descriptions of a tall, blond, English-looking man; of a young American man named Peter Macdonald.

Meanwhile, CCF soldiers and U.S. Marines from Georgia and Florida search the beaches, the grasslands, even the island's large, steamy rain forest: West Hills.

An exhaustive house-by-house, hotel-by-hotel search is begun in the cities of Coastown, Port Gerry, and Cape John.

Also, every nationality represented on the Elizabeth's Fancy bus sends some kind of special help. These are: Germany: the U.S.; England; Canada; France; Israel; Trinidad; Jamaica; Argentina; Texas.

Ballistics, riot, and interrogation experts are hurried in from New York City and Washington. More federal marshals are flown in to help keep order in the cities. Headhunters—including a special team called "Czech" —come from as far away as Eastern Europe. Bounties totaling over $150,000 are set.

Learning that "an English-looking man" is being sought, a small group is set up at Interpol's Secretariat in St.-Cloud, France. Information on known gunrunners and mercenaries is collated and sent out from Interpol's Criminal Records Department. Extensive checks are made on the dead men, Kingfish Toone and the Cuban, Blinkie Tomas.

Through all of this, Campbell and Harold Hill's "lead" on the Roses is never once questioned. Even the bitterest of police-world cynics wouldn't speculate and come up with what has actually happened in the Caribbean.

By early night of the first day, the hunt has turned up eight tall blond men. Two-thirds of the twelve.

Looking in on the eight—all between six foot two and six foot four; all blond; all handsome as hell—Federal Marshal Stuart Leedman of Los Angeles gets the feeling that somebody isn't telling him everything he needs to know about this grisly case. Something is as fishy as San Diego Sea World, Stu Leedman is thinking.

"Now what do you do for a living?" he asks Antoine Coffey, a wispy blond who has listed his address as the World of Free Spirits.

The blond model seems confused by the question.

"A living?"

"Yeah," Stu Leedman says. "What do you do for money, Antoine? How do you pay the rent? Get money to go to the movies?"

Coffey smiles suddenly. "Oh, *that*," he whispers. "Thhodomy, you mean."

Marshal Stuart Leedman stands up in the quiet examination room and screams at the open door.

"Who ordered in all of these blond faggots?" His voice carries up and down the serene, dignified hallways of the U.S. Embassy. "What the *fuck, Jesus Christ, shit* is going on around this pisshole?"

It's every bit as maddening and confusing as the machete murders themselves. More so, because it comes on top of them . . . Which is exactly the way Damian wants it.

Port Gerry, San Dominica

TUESDAY EVENING

His nose pressed against the cool green glass of the Number 9 bus window, Peter watches a row of flowered shirts drift by on Station Street. Stranger in Paradise, he thinks.

He sees pink and purple shirts like the Spanish in big cities always wear. Leather mushroom caps and tiny fedoras. Black wraparound sunglasses. San Dominican country boys trying to look like the Tonton Macoute.

People seem to be forever waiting for buses around San Dominica, Peter has begun to notice. The Elizabeth's Fancy bus massacre is mind-blowing when you think about it like that. It's like attacking an Interstate Highway in the United States. Severing a main artery.

Black women in homemade dresses and sandals are pressed up closer to the station. A nest of young conchie girls. "Queen bees" they call them around Coastown.

As the Number 9 bus starts to brake, Macdonald puts his hand on the Colt .44 under his shirt. His heart starts to thump. . . . Peter has begun to imagine the tall blond man waiting around every corner, behind every palm tree. Like some slick, handsome bogey-man. Waiting just for him . . .

The bus station is a wooden shack covered with antique beer and Coke signs worth more than the building itself.

Stopping in front, the Number 9 bucks and shivers like an old belly dancer. All the people and livestock being transported inside wake up suddenly.

Chickens squawk and flap red and white wings like feather dusters. A goat starts kicking the seats and an old black man starts kicking the goat.

"Ay maum in dat blue dress!" a Rude Boy shouts out a bus window.

There's a loud *wooshing* of steaming hot air, and the driver says something Macdonald can't follow. People start walking off the bus though, and Peter guesses that he's there.

This hole-in-the-wall must be the summer capital city of Port Gerry.

Eating a thirty-cent meat pie from the station canteen, Peter climbs a dark street with no sidewalks. With dreary two- and three-story limestone buildings on either side of him.

The pie smells like halitosis; the street smells like human sweat. Peter's body feels as if it might collapse pretty soon. . . . The last time he remembers feeling so bad is when he'd had dysentery in Thailand.

He's feeling lonely as hell too. Thinking about Jane constantly.

The first time he'd seen her at the Plantation Inn, he'd thought she was trouble. Quiet—only with a bad dose of New York City smug . . . Quick wiseass front. Shooting down every guy who said hello to her at the inn. In Peter's mind, she was a blond version of Ali McGraw. Trouble. . . . One weekend, though, he'd asked her if she wanted to go on a cross-island trip with him. See the West Hills jungle. See the beaches on the other side. And surprise! She said sure. . . . Twenty-four hours later, the two of them still hadn't stopped talking. An amazing day of straight talk about one another. Striking chords in each other like crazy. Strangers practically. Crying together before the first day was over. Huddled together on a dark, deserted beach called Runaway . . . Because they'd both been so damn lonely. Because there'd been so many things they'd wanted to tell somebody. . . .

Halfway up the hill, Peter sees a sign that says RENT. Another sign says ROOMS, and shows a little black angel sleeping on folded hands.

A doorway at the crest of the hill says WELCOME, and that seems just about right to Peter.

A tall, goateed man and a boy sit at a buckling table in the foyer covered with dominoes.

"Yes, mon?" The older fellow speaks. A soft, serious voice. Much more businesslike than Peter expected from the look of the place outside.

"I need a room please. I'm very tired."

The black man looks at Peter strangely. Shrugs. Then he goes to a little school desk where he scrawls a line in a red ledger. He takes six dollars in advance for the room.

"Dis bway will take yo' up. Yo' be served breakfas' in de mornin', mon."

The young boy points to a dark stairway. Then he walks ahead of Macdonald, holding a candle in a soup dish.

The boy begins to whisper to Peter as they climb the stairs. His small candle slowly reveals the hotel, like a murder mystery.

"T'marra yo' cum fishin' in me fadder boat, mon. Catch grouper. Lotsa big snappers too."

Peter suddenly starts to laugh at the top of the stairs.

"I'm sorry." He turns to the boy. "I'm not laughing at you. I can't go fishing tomorrow, though."

"Too bad, mon. Yo' missin' good shit."

Peter and the black boy turn into a slanting, lop-sided hallway with unpainted doors on both sides of a long, tattered runner. A dim light shines at the other end of the hall. A black telephone sits on the floor under the light. Suddenly Peter understands that this is an all-black hotel. *Welcome.*

Inside his room, he hides his wallet between the rusty pipes of the sink.

He bumps his head hard on the pipes and feels strangely, ridiculously exhilarated. For a minute, he even forgets about the Tall Blond Man. The Butcher.

Then Peter just sits in bed with his head propped up so he faces the door. With the Colt revolver lying across his boxer shorts. Listening to the ricky-tick rhythms of reggae out in the streets; listening to pigs rooting in the hotel's backyard.

Before he can sleep, he has the urge to go back out into the moldy hallway.

He picks up the black telephone and asks for Number 107. He gets through to a night operator with a beautiful lilting voice. Nightbird. Then to a groggy, very distant-sounding woman. Then to Jane.

"Hiya, Laurel." Peter's face lights up with a sleepy smile. "This is Oliver Hardy speaking. I think I'm going crazy, babe. . . ."

Our strategy for Brooks Campbell was a simple one: we tried to give him too many choices and produce decision stress. Harold Hill was a completely different problem. We went right for Hill's balls.

The Rose Diary

Fairfax Station, Virginia

At 2:30 in the morning, two Virginia state troopers, James Walsh and Dominick Niccolo, tramp across the dewy back lawns of a big white house way out in the sticks.

A nearby neighbor has reported something strange going on at the house. What sounded like screams for help.

Around at the back, the policemen discover that the kitchen door isn't locked. Not all that unusual for the rural community of Fairfax Station. Not usual though, either.

Inside the kitchen they're greeted with the loud ticking of an electric clock. The hum of a refrigerator. The indistinct sounds of an empty, or sleeping, house.

The kitchen is lit by an orangish night light over the sink.

Several coffee cups and half a box of Dunkin' Donuts

are sitting out on the kitchen table. The remains of half a dozen sandwiches.

Dom Niccolo turns on the hall light and calls out in a high-pitched tenor's voice.

"Hello. Is anyone home? This is the Virginia State Police."

No answer.

The two men continue to walk through the dark house, turning on lights as they go. Calling out, "Is anyone home?"

A standing lamp in the living room is already on.

As they enter the comfortably furnished room, they're startled by the loud crashing of the refrigerator making ice.

"That son of a bitch." James Walsh grits his teeth.

The troopers hear another noise and a young black retriever comes running downstairs, wagging its tail and jumping up on the two men, licking them.

"Pup scared the shit out of me too." Walsh grins.

"Jesus Christ, Jimmy." Dom Niccolo kneels to look closer at the dog. "She has blood all over her side. Look at this, Jimmy."

Both men unholster their sidearms.

"This is the Virginia State Police!" Niccolo calls from the foot of the stairs.

"We better get some more help here," Walsh whispers.

Niccolo motions for him to shut up. "Come on."

Dominick Niccolo, then James Walsh, head up the shag-carpeted stairway. Both men have their guns pointed up into the dark hallway above.

Right at the top of the stairs they find a woman.

Carole Hill is barefoot, dressed in a flowered blouse and white walking shorts. Blood is caked on her face and chest. A pool is shining on the carpet beside her.

Two bedrooms down the hall, James Walsh finds a teen-age boy.

Mark Hill is inside his own clothes closet. The boy is gagged and tied up with a telephone wire. But at least he's alive.

In the master bedroom, Dominick Niccolo is calling the trooper barracks in Alexandria.

"The house is on Shad Stream Road," he says into a pink Princess telephone. "Belongs to Mr. and Mrs. Harold Hill. The husband doesn't seem to be here. . . . Johnny, you won't believe this, but there's a three-foot machete stuck in that poor woman's heart. Jimmy Walsh is up here puking in the hallway. Hurry up, will you? . . ."

The machete murders have come to America. Almost to Langley. Just fourteen miles from the White House.

The warning couldn't have been any clearer.

May 7, 1975, Wednesday

STALK
TALL
BLOND
MAN

From the Rose Diary

In December of 1974, I had wired, then telephoned, our last important player—an expensive English shooter named Clive Lawson. At that time, Lawson was buying and selling cocaine and four-star pornography in North Miami Beach, Florida.

During our eventual phone conversation, I told Lawson that Señor Miguel Alvarez of Caracas (Pietra Forte) and Anthony Patriarca of Miami (Cosa Nostra) were my sponsors; that I was interested in purchasing a large stock of 16-millimeter films I heard he had, or could get.

"Do you have anything that might stimulate older gentlemen?" I asked him over the phone. "Large, private screenings for older gentlemen?"

Lawson said that he might have something. He didn't know. He didn't do business over the phone.

On the fifteenth of December, we met in the very unlikely Poodle Bar at the Fontainebleau Hotel.

For our meeting, the English killer was wearing a wrinkled white shirt. A funky plaid sports jacket.

Thick, black-rimmed glasses that were so square-looking I couldn't quite believe them. . . . Because, you see, Clive Lawson was an exceptionally handsome man. A little like Michael Caine from a distance. A lot like Damian.

He ordered Tanqueray with a twist, and I had something chic like Campari. Both of us played our parts for a while, then I simply announced to him that I was Carrie Rose.

After that admission, we talked about the Congo and Southeast Asia—places where we'd both worked and vaguely heard of one another. We talked about how Clive had fallen into the pornography business through the Pietra Forte—the so-called Latin-American Connection. We talked about Damian and myself.

Then, as factually yet vaguely as possible, I explained something about San Dominica to the English killer.

"As a further introduction," I said at the end of my opening gambit, "I have to tell you that we can't let anyone in on the total picture down there. Like who holds the contract. That's rule number one. . . . On the other hand, we're offering very large fees for peripheral work that shouldn't be all that hard."

The green eyes behind Lawson's black-rimmed glasses sparkled like large emeralds. He had a relaxed, confident manner that I was beginning to like. "My favorite sort of work," he said. "Do go on."

"For one week in May," I continued, "your job will be to lead the San Dominican police on a wild-goose chase all over the island. That's where your time in the Congo fits in nicely for our purposes. It's also where you earn your money."

Lawson's eyebrows arched a little.

"Will I be shooting at people? Or getting shot at?"

"If you're careless, you'll get shot, I'm sure. The usual ground rules apply, Clive. There will be at least two hits for you. Probably military targets. Lower-echelon assholes."

The tall blond man smiled. He understood perfectly. At least he thought he understood: he was to run cover for our escape.

"How much?" he asked next.

"Fifty thousand dollars."

Lawson started to laugh. "No haggling, ay? I don't even get a chance to try and bargain you up. All right, I think so. . . . How about sixty? I assume I have to get my own behind out of there. . . ."

"Sixty is fine."

"Money in advance, of course."

"Of course."

I laid it right out in front of the English killer. A fat brown envelope on the Fontainebleau bar.

. . . Damian and I had just purchased one of the most expensive pigeon in the history of crime. One of the keys to our getting away with murder.

On the morning of May 7, 1975—Wednesday—we let our pigeon fly. We had Clive Lawson make a big kill, while impersonating Damian.

Behind every successful woman, there's a big prick.

The Rose Diary

May 7, 1975; Coastown, San Dominica

WEDNESDAY MORNING, THE NINTH DAY OF THE SEASON

Harold Hill hadn't slept well the night of the sixth.

At 5:30 in the morning, he calls Brooks Campbell's home in Coastown. Yet another bizarre phone call for poor Campbell.

"We have to get that kid Macdonald," Hill blurts out with no introduction whatsoever—as if he and Campbell had been carrying on the conversation all night. "For all we know now, we could have Damian Rose locked up already. We can't identify him by ourselves."

Brooks Campbell tries to wake himself up in a hurry. Hill is saying something that sounds important. Hill is saying something. . . .

"We, uhh . . . need someone who knows what Rose looks like," Campbell finally manages.

"Exactly," Harold Hill says. "So let's concentrate on Macdonald as much as we can today."

. . . The configurations change a little at 8:00 A.M. At eight, Langley reaches Hill with the news about his wife.

Langley doesn't understand, though. *Carole Hill's murder doesn't make any sense.*

Harry the Hack understands. Either he gets Damian Rose, or Damian Rose gets him.

Port Gerry, San Dominica

That morning, Peter wakes with the bright Caribbean sun streaming in two windows, exploding on a shaving mirror nailed over the sink.

A doctorbird stands on one of the window sills, pecking at wood splinters. . . . The velvet, skullcapped head eyes the sleepy-faced man coldly, sneezes, then resumes its noisy woodworking.

"Hey. Be sociable or beat it," Peter says to the bird. He's feeling better—okay, human anyway. Something about the hotel room, all the sunlight probably, the nearby water, reminds him of his family's place up on Lake Michigan.

In daylight, the hotel is both pleasant and pleasantly ridiculous. There are different patterns of tacky wallpaper on three of the four walls, for example—but he can also see a wide lane of cheery blue sea without getting out of bed.

"God, throw me a crumb," Peter whispers to the open window.

Sitting yogi style on the rumpled gray sheets, the ex-West Point man in him writes out a formal battle plan

213

on the back of a single postcard he finds in the night-stand.

Rockefeller resort (Caneel Bay).
Fly Martinique? St. Thomas?
New York City . . . transfer to Washington.
Senator Pflanzer. State Department? Washington Post?
Janie flight out.
Fish 'n Fool.

The Great Escape . . . The pretty good escape, anyway.

There's a sharp rap at the hotel-room door and Peter's stomach does a dramatic elevator-shaft drop. He grabs hold of the Colt .44 under his bed sheets.

A pretty brown girl with a full breakfast tray peeks into the room. "Breakfus, sir."

"Oh, man." Peter moans. "I just woke up about thirty seconds ago." He tries to smile. "It's okay. C'mon."

The girl has brought white toast with no crust. Enough marmalade and guava jelly for several loaves of bread. Plus steaming coffee in a child's thermos that shows cartoon pigs and a leering wolf.

Peter can see the tips of the girl's breasts as she puts down the food. Pretty, swaying breasts. Pretty brown legs. A nice, maidenish bum.

The girl's thin brown hands move smoothly on the plastic dishes.

Watching her work, it occurs to Peter that he hasn't really spoken to anyone in a day and a half—not in person, anyway. *Hi, there,* he hears several times in his mind. *I'm feeling a little nuts right now. Sit down. Have some of your good coffee there. . . .*

Peter says nothing, though.

He watches the girl walk back across the room. A

truly lovely little ass, heartbreaking smile—travel-poster material.

"Your breakfus gettin' cold." She smiles at the door. Then she leaves Peter chewing his toast, watching the songbird, unexpectedly hard and alive.

And a little more afraid because of it.

Shortly after eleven, he changes into a secondhand muslin work shirt; brown chinos; a floppy blue hat. It's a working disguise Peter hopes will work just one more time for him.

At quarter past, he leaves the tiny hotel—the Welcome. Off to find a boat called the *Fish 'n Fool*.

Peter knows that the boat regularly brings guests back and forth from the expensive Rockefeller resort at Caneel Bay. From Caneel Bay, he can take a prop plane to another island with safe flight connections to New York and Washington. Once he's in Washington . . . well, at least he won't be in San Dominica. Someone is going to listen to him and Jane in Washington. His father has an old friend, for one thing—Senator Pflanzer. Peter himself knows an Army general at the Pentagon. . . .

It's going to be weird when it hits the fan in America, Peter starts to think. It's going to be devastating, in fact.

Whoever hired the blond mercenary at Turtle Bay is in for a hell of a big surprise.

Around 12:15, Peter is floating on a pure adrenaline high.

It's close to the feeling he'd always gotten on afternoon patrols in Asia. No Man's Nam. Where he'd invented new ways to block out as much shit as possible. To drift. Go with the flow.

All the world a little grainy, he's concentrating hard on a handsome black dude collecting stubs at the stern of the *Fish 'n Fool*. The dude is wearing a shocking-pink T-shirt; short-shorts; tightly wound coral bracelets and a necklace. He doesn't look as if he'll be any trouble, but Peter braces himself anyway.

"*Parlez-vous français?*" He grins big baby-grand piano teeth at Peter. "Nope. You're American, right?"

"New York City. West Sixty-third Street." Peter lies so automatically, acts so well, it scares him a little. "We leave around twelve-thirty?"

"Twelve-thirty on the button." The young black keeps his smile like a good trouser crease. "Give or take five minutes or a half hour for some of my lost *turista* friends . . . John Sampson, Norfawk, Virginah." The man puts out his hand. He widens his smile another 15 percent. "At your beck and call, New York."

Peter finally smiles back at the man. *A pseudo-fag! Jesus.* He tilts his floppy hat down and walks up on the main deck.

The afterdeck of the *Fish 'n Fool* is all polished brass and rich mahogany.

It's jam-packed with bronze gods and goddesses. With designer-signed T-shirts and Parisian jeans; $40 sunglasses; the smells of benzocaine, camphor, hot, burning flesh.

"Hi." *Long black hair. Jet-set tan. A red string bikini.*

"How are you?" Peter smiles. Feels like the boat's chaplain.

"Hyellow!" *Frizzy, short blond hair. Mirror sunglasses. A man.*

"Hyellow."

Seeming bashful if anything, cutely backwards, Macdonald makes his way to a padded bench half in, half out of the sun. He's a little self-conscious about his hair —shaggy for him; about the inescapable fact that he smells after his days on the road.

He puts his tennis sneakers up on the brass rail. Pulls the floppy hat down over his eyes. Listens to the quick beat of his good, strong heart.

Tomorrow's going to be so unreal, he thinks. *Washington. No idea exactly where he'll start yet.*

Then, very slowly, Peter drifts far, far away from it all. To a pretty, half-awake place with no guns, no machetes, no slick blond killers. *Just Janie. Rest. Escape.*

In the meantime, the black dude, John Sampson, from Norfolk, Virginia, is up on shore making a phone call.

At 1:15, the sky is a roaring fire fight. Flame-throwers. An entire South Vietnamese city on fire.

The hat is still over his face, but Peter's eyes are open wide. He's trying to see through the loose weave of the summer fabric.

For a long moment, it's almost as if he's inside a large, packed, American sports arena. A low crowd murmur echoes all around him. Like he's sitting in the bleachers during a brief lull in a dramatic World Series game. Tiger Stadium. Mickey Lolich on the mound. Everything but the hot-dog men . . .

"Mr. Macdonald."

Crowd murmur.

"Good afternoon, Peter."

Crowd murmur.

Clammy and dry-tongued, with a disgustingly sour taste in his mouth, Peter slides back the hat.

He isn't properly prepared to believe the things he sees in the blinding sunlight.

A crowd, largely blacks, is being held back on the dock by CDS soldiers. Fifty people, maybe a hundred, are all straining to watch the *Fish 'n Fool.*

Policemen carrying old-fashioned rifles are running single file onto the yacht.

Close up, Macdonald tries to focus on John Sampson from Norfolk, Virginia. Then on the island police chief. On a gray-haired American man he doesn't recognize. Finally, on Brooks Campbell. White linen suit. Horn-rimmed sunglasses that are too big for him. Handsome as ever . . .

Suddenly, Peter is very tired, unbelievably weary. His head begins to swim like feeding time in a fish tank; his heart beats so hard and fast it scares the living shit out of him.

"Good afternoon," Campbell repeats.

"You have to come with us," the black police chief says. "There's nothing to worry about."

Now there's a Bob Hope one-liner that should have gotten a laugh, Peter thinks. Instead, he just blinks at the four men. His mind reeling like three windows in a slot machine . . . *Blond Englishmen, Colonel Dred, Cosa Nostra. Not going to get to Washington. Senator Pflanzer* . . .

"Give you a hand, Macdonald."

Grubby, light-bearded, he gets up by himself.

All the jet-setters on the deck are standing around watching now. Whispering in one another's ears how they'd thought he looked funny when he came on board.

Tourists are aiming fancy cameras into Peter's face. Stupid, grinning bastards. Grinning soldiers with dull black rifles—phony guns that look as if they've been carved out of soap.

Campbell and the other American man walking right beside him. A very official-looking march. Leading him through the tunnel of ambulance chasers. The other man trying to introduce himself . . . ". . . [something] Hill . . ." Trying to shake Peter's hand.

Then, in the middle of the mad crowd, in the middle of everything, the police chief suddenly swings Peter around. The sweating, heavyset black man stares him right in the face, looks pained and sensitive and a little crazy himself.

"Strange, unaccountable things are still happening on our island," Meral Johnson says to Peter. The man seems to pause out of confusion, then tears start down over the rolls of his cheeks.

"Jane Cooke was killed this morning," Johnson whispers to Peter. "I'm very sorry, mister."

Mandeville, San Dominica

At quarter to ten that morning, two short-haired men in conservative gray suits had taken Jane—in a wheelchair—out a rear-door exit in the Mandeville Hospital.

As the chair whistled along a flowery path with royal palms and plumbago everywhere, the pretty blond girl was starting to smile again. Laughing for the first time in years, it seemed.

"Reminds me of Bermuda a little," one of the men was saying.

"Reminds me a little of *Ironside*," Jane mumbled a small joke.

The man pushing her wheelchair laughed through his nose. He was James McGuire, fifty-nine, a paunchy, good-natured sort who reminded Jane of Santa Claus with no white beard.

The second man, James Dowd, was just thirty-one. James Dowd was quieter than McGuire, but very nice. Very old-world Irish.

When the wheelchair was out of sight of Mandeville Hospital, deep in rich green brush, James McGuire stopped pushing.

"Okay, Janie." The red-faced man grinned. "You

want to walk, you most surely can walk. You don't want to ride. I sure as heck don't want to push."

As the three Americans continued down the path, walking, they began to see more and more colorful birds. Plus lizards, tree frogs, hermit crabs. An ornery little mongoose looking for a snake in the grass.

Then the winding path they were on ended abruptly in a flat, breezy field.

Jane, even the two FBI inspectors, let out short gasps of delight and awe. Beyond the field was nothing but shining, royal-blue sea.

"You know, I don't think I could be anything but happy in a beautiful place like this." James Dowd finally entered the chitchatting. "I know that isn't strictly logical."

"That's how you're going to get trapped into staying here." Jane smiles at the shy, likable man. "You'll quit your job and . . . James!"

Without a sound of warning, three men suddenly appear from behind thick brush and rocks. They wear green windbreakers and sportshirts buttoned to the throat.

"Freeze!" one of them screams.

At the same time, another man starts to fire an Uzi submachine gun. A tall blond man.

Both Dowd and McGuire fall over backwards into high grass. Then two of the men jump on Jane. One holds down her flailing arms; the other presses a wet handkerchief over her nose, mouth, across strands of her long, curly hair.

Understanding that it's all going to happen again, feeling as if she's on the edge of madness, Jane begins to let loose amazing screams she wouldn't have believed possible.

They're putting the dripping cloth all over her face and she's trying to bite the hand holding it. They're pushing her head back hard into the ground.

Finally, her arm snaps under a man's heavy leg.

Then everything is the suffocating white cloth. Its acrid, choking smell. Like trying to breathe inside a bottle of glue.

She starts to give in to it finally. Blue sky, sun, angry or frightened faces flashing over her. *The blond Englishman. Here* . . . She thinks of Peter. Starts to cry. Feels like a helpless child under their arms, legs, stomachs . . .

Then Jane bites down hard into a man's ugly, bulbous thumb.

"Don't fight. Jesus Christ," one of the men is yelling at her.

"Christ. She's biting my fucking hand!" the second man screams.

Hospital people—white-coated doctors, nurses—finally appear on the far side of the field.

Which is when Clive Lawson bends and shoots the struggling young woman in the right temple.

Jane thinks it's the Tall Blond Man bent over her. Not quite as good-looking as she'd thought . . . She wants to hold Peter just one more time. Then it all seems so stupid and awful. . . . Then it's nothing at all.

DRAGNET TIGHT. THOUSANDS STOPPED

The part I was supposed to play around Washington and Europe from the sixth to the ninth was no part, really. It was all the things I thought I wanted to become. . . . Sitting in the Gralyn Hotel. Watching a college boy eat a sandwich outside. Thinking that Port-Smithe is nearly perfect. Thinking about the Loner from Coastown. About Nickie Handy. Damian . . . Bizarre thoughts. Like whether I'll be alive one year from this exact moment. . . . Am I?

The Rose Diary

May 8, 1975; Washington, D.C.

THURSDAY MORNING, THE TENTH DAY OF THE SEASON

At 10:00 A.M. San Dominica time, nine o'clock in Washington, Mrs. Susan Chaplin sits out in the charming garden café of the Gralyn Hotel on N Street.

Mrs. Chaplin wears a cream blouse with matching scarf; a navy skirt; blue and white spectators; big sunglasses pushed back on her hair.

She's toying with warm baking-powder biscuits, creamed finnan haddie, and a London prostitute who goes by the stage name Betsy Port-Smithe.

Mrs. Susan Chaplin is the stage name for Carrie Rose.

"What I have in mind," Carrie is explaining, watching a Washington hippie eat an impossibly stuffed Blimpie on the other side of beautifully sculpted hedges, "is a little, uhm, unusual. . . ."

"Unusual?" Port-Smithe shrugs. "Well, let's see. I'm too young, and good, to get beat up for it. That means *any* sum of money, Mrs. Chaplin . . . What is unusual?" The tall, sandy-haired woman starts to laugh. "You want me to pop out of a charlotte chantilly at someone's fund-raising dinner?"

Carrie Rose begins to laugh too.

When Port-Smithe keeps giggling, some of the other patrons of the garden café begin to sneak glances at the two of them.

The young women are framed against a background of plain green umbrellas and the beginnings of Georgetown. Both look very much a part of the expensive, former Embassy scene at the Gralyn. From the look of them, the two women might even be sisters. The resemblance is startling.

An attentive waiter slips away their breakfast plates (fish, bran flakes, porridge). He inserts plump grapes and shiny pears.

"Some time in the next week," Carrie (Mrs. Chaplin) continues, when the laughing has stopped, "my husband, Damian, is due to arrive here in Washington.

"He's coming directly from an obnoxious, hectic, brutal series of business conferences in the Caribbean. . . . Damian sells clothes. Expensive women's clothes.

"At any rate, for some private reasons, I can't be here to meet him. At least I can't *wait* around here for the entire week. . . ."

Port-Smithe sits with a plump grape ready to be popped into her pouty mouth. "And? . . ."

"I'd like you to meet Damian for me. . . . I'd like you to meet him at the St. James, and stay with him a night if I'm not here. That's all."

"Do you know how much I might charge?" Betsy Port-Smithe asks. "For a week of waiting around?"

"I don't. But I'll pay you two hundred a day. Plus your room at the St. James. Plus your food . . . You're free as a bird until Damian comes. You can even work, if you like. I mean, I realize you're very good, Betsy. That's the whole idea."

The London call girl smiles. She thinks that she has it figured out now. . . . This prissy young American wife is looking for some kind of ménage. She just doesn't have the nerve to ask for it. . . . *Well, fine and dandy*.

"To Damian." Port-Smithe raises a cup of coffee with *eau de vie*.

"To Damian." Carrie Rose smiles demurely. She's beginning to get a very good feeling about the way things are breaking on her side of the partnership.

That afternoon she has to fly out of Dulles International.

To Zurich.

To money, power, and those wonderful little Munchkins who make the world run so fast and furiously.

Carrie is well aware that she has only one day left now. Approximately thirty hours to outwit several self-acclaimed geniuses, all of them male.

Coastown, San Dominica

They had carefully hidden Peter Macdonald in an expensive suite at the posh Coastown Golf & Racquet Condominiums.

A minimum of five CIA operatives—top men in the Caribbean Account—eat, sleep, and read *Penthouse* and Alistair MacLean novels in the seven-room suite with him.

As many as eight agents are there the first day. Three times that many ride pink-canopied golf carts around the manicured lawns all through the night. It's an accepted fact that it will take an army to get Macdonald out of there alive.

Up to his chest in steaming pink-marble bath water, Peter floats quietly in one of the three condominium bathrooms.

There's a strange feeling in his head. . . . He'd actually felt his mind go *snap* Wednesday afternoon.

Standing beside the *Fish 'n Fool,* the black policeman holding him by both shoulders, loud-whispering, "Jane was killed this morning. I'm very sorry, mister."

Snap.

Like breaking a bone, tearing a tendon. Never knowing before that his head had been so fragile.

It isn't exactly that he won't be able to exist without Janie. He will. Has for twenty-odd years before he met her . . . It's more that he doesn't think he can be completely sane without her. . . .

Sane is something he'd never been particularly good at anyway. *Sane*. Coping; content; not painfully lonely; not jumping into West Point because you think it will make your father love you.

Six-fifteen A.M. on his old Timex. Ten days since it all began.

Red sun shooting streaks through a louvered bathroom window.

Somebody already playing tennis outside . . . *Bonk . . . bonk . . . bonk* . . . Undoubtedly more agents . . .

They'd tried awfully hard to be nice. The San Dominican police. CIA. They'd left him pretty much by himself the night before. Not bugged him with too many questions . . .

He'd sat alone in a dark bedroom in the condominium most of the night. Big New York–cut steak untouched on a tray. Asparagus tips. Strawberry parfait sundae. Feeling like a little kid left alone in a big house. Having some kind of bizarre Kodachrome-quality memory of the first time he and Janie had been together. A three-day cross-island trip while they were still practically strangers. The kind of great, dopey, romantic stuff that could only happen in a vacation spot. Making him cry, he missed her so badly . . .

Peter turns his body in the hot, soapy tub. The hot water feels unreal in the rush of air conditioning. Like lying under covers with the window open in winter . . . Everything weird, and unreal, and impossible to relate to.

His mind has just gone snap. Snap, crackle, pop.

Peter doesn't give a shit. He does; but he doesn't.

What he wants now—what he's been thinking abou
since late last night—is how he can get his revenge.
Everything so beautifully simple, for a change. Just one
guiding light. Get the blond mercenary somehow. Blow
his brains out. Just like Jane, only slower.

Sitting in the bathtub, Peter figures out one other
important thing. He figures that he probably won't
have to worry about looking for the Blond Englishman.

One day he'll look up—and the blond man will just
be there. Just like at Turtle Bay.

At nine o'clock, Damian sits inside a Coastown church and carefully studies the place. A small black boy comes up to him and Damian makes the most horrifying face he can imagine. The boy laughs like a banshee. Visitors in the church turn to complain, then they begin to smile too.

Meanwhile, the hired English killer is accelerating the merry, wild-mouse chase around San Dominica.

He's also managing to round out Damian's flat and until then rather bloodless character. Clive Lawson is getting Rose labeled as a first-class pervert.

Sitting on one of the stonework terraces of the ramshackle Royal Caribbean Hotel, Lawson eyes a cocky little stinkpot chugging up toward Coastown under big mackerel clouds.

In a dilapidated white-wicker chair two feet across from him, a naked, mewing seventeen-year-old is expounding some sort of psychedelic Swami-Moon-Castaneda gibberish about organic orgasms.

The adult-breasted teen has gray streaks in very

long black hair. Her face is long too, spare and striking.

"Like . . . like saffron and ocher paints . . . are like mixing on the insides of my eyelids," she says in a whispery voice that makes the revelation sexy if nothing else.

Meanwhile, she's sticking two long fingers deep inside herself.

Clive Lawson watches the girl's fingers work back and forth, back and forth, like two long legs walking in dune grass. Very slowly, he masturbates himself with both hands.

The girl's name is Stormy Lascher. Half of her brain has been blasted away by acid and psilocybin; the other half departed while she was working at a massage parlor inside New York's once mediocre Commodore Hotel.

The blond Englishman, she's discovering—chauvinist and dirty old thirty-three-year-old that he is—also has an interesting (blue-veined, cocky-hatted, well-muscled) Capricorn prick. In fact, his standard equipment compares favorably with the slimmer, cuter rocketships on so many of the college boys from nearby Sunshower Beach.

"I'm going to come any sec," the seventeen-year-old screams, pointing her dirty silver-toed feet up like a ballet dancer. "Oh, Jesus. Jesus Christ."

Stormy starts to shiver, moan, and she brings a long tab of amyl nitrate up to her little pug nose.

As she breaks open the tab, she hears the blond man say very clearly, "I'm the one they're looking for. The Englishman. Now there's one for your record book, Storm."

The long-haired girl nods her head once—then nothing but bright, mixing paints are there any more.

By 10:00 A.M., the English killer is on the road up

232

to Coastown, heading toward another of his targets.

By ten, Denise "Stormy" Lascher is sitting out on the terrace of Room 334, screaming like the hopeless madwoman she'll one day become.

At a little after eleven, the police, the Army, and the CIA swarm over the Royal Caribbean like ants on a gingerbread castle. Harold Hill and Brooks Campbell march through the ornate front lobby together, Campbell carrying a bulky M-16 rifle. The police stop all regular elevator service, and begin to search the ancient, sprawling dinosaur from the cellar up to the gabled rooftops.

Hill, Campbell, and Dr. Johnson go directly to room 334, where Denise Lascher is being detained.

The hysterical teen-ager tells them that the man must have left before all the police came busting in. She doesn't know for sure. . . . Yes, he was tall. Blondhaired. Like Michael Caine, she says . . . No, she doesn't remember anything specific he'd said. Just that he was the one. . . . The machete killer everyone is looking for.

Harold Hill rummages through the trash baskets in the suite's bedroom and bath. The gray-haired CIA director finds empty, crushed packs of Dunhill cigarettes, marijuana roaches, an empty carton for Remington rifle shells, a box for French ticklers. Garbage.

Meanwhile, Meral Johnson has put out an alert for the car the tall blond man has been seen driving. A blue 1974 Mustang; license number 3984-A according to the hotel register.

Johnson sends his men and the American inspectors around the hotel to interview as many of the guests and help as possible. At the same time, he has roadblocks set up outside Carolinsted; all through the surrounding villages.

Dr. Johnson has the feeling that they might finally be closing in on him. The black man hasn't slept for two days now; he's obsessed with getting the blond mercenary. More so than any of them, he believes privately . . . Johnson alone understands that the Tall Blond Man has destroyed San Dominica.

In front of the hotel, Campbell and Harold Hill lean on a driftwood fence railing, both of them chain-smoking.

"I haven't known what to say about Carole." Campbell flips his cigarette out onto the beach sand. "I'm sorry. I hope you know how I feel, Harry."

"You feel that you have to say something," Harold Hill says, and smiles cruelly. "That's all you feel, Brooks."

Campbell lets his eyes drift out over the soothing, beautiful Caribbean.

"What about Macdonald?"

"If we catch Rose, Macdonald makes the ID. I'd hate to do it off that photokit drawing. . . . I'm also prepared to try him as bait for Rose. If we can be clever enough to do that discreetly."

"I think Rose might try to hit Macdonald anyway. What else is keeping him around here?"

Harold Hill extends his hands, palms up. He doesn't know.

The two men walk back across the hotel's rolling lawns. As they approach a waiting Puma helicopter, men in blue jumpsuits begin to take off the plane's chocks and hawsers.

"We're getting very close to him now," Harold Hill says. "Or vice versa."

At eleven o'clock, Peter makes the first of four tape recordings for the CIA's over 8,500,000,000-item computer files.

For an hour and a half straight, he talks into a reel-to-reel Sony for the edification of two very hip academic-type interrogators from Washington. He tells them about his odyssey through the West Hills jungle; about everything he'd seen at Turtle Bay; about his feelings toward the U.S. government after Watergate; after Cambodia; after, say, he'd killed his first North Vietnamese; after, say, Jane had been killed. . . .

In short, the two interrogators are trying to determine whether Peter is going to give them any trouble.

At 12:30, a police artist starts a photokit drawing of Damian Rose based on what Peter can remember from the unbelievable fifteen-second tableau on the Shore Highway.

By one o'clock, his interrogators are in the offices of Alcoa Aluminum, color-Xeroxing a fair likeness of the tall blond man.

Also at one o'clock, Peter asks the CIA for a gun to protect himself, but he is refused.

At two, a crowd of agents remove him from the Golf & Racquet Condominiums. Things going too fast all of a sudden. Everything fuzzy and unclear.

They take an elevator two floors down to the lobby. Then a fast walk through a garden—to a gray Ford with little American flags on the fenders.

Switch back two cars to a blue Mercury Cougar with the shiniest front grille in captivity. A car smiling like rich suburban kids with braces.

Doors shut like clockwork, then the blue Mercury jerks away from the curb. Flashes past palm trees and stately casuarinas. Tires screeching out onto Orange Boulevard, where unconcerned blacks sell bananas and papaya on the sidewalks.

Off to the Church of the Angels. Off to see a lot of the victims, including Jane.

Sitting in back—arms folded, mind folded—Peter wonders why they've decided to go to the church in broad daylight. He forgets the thought momentarily. Sees Jane blinking on and off like neon lights. Sees the blond man over Turtle Bay. Sees himself on the flashy yellow Peugeot bicycle.

"You all right, Pete?"

"Yeah. Sure. I was just thinking. . . ."

Inside the medium-sized Catholic church, Harold Hill and Brooks Campbell wait in the sacristy. Both Washington men are wearing lightweight business suits; they look appropriately respectful.

They're discussing important logistics with an oblate priest, Father Kevin Brennan. Like where all the side and back doors are. Where the press can get their photographs but not get in the way. Where an assassin

—"If an assassin has it in mind, Father"—might try to hide inside the church.

Meanwhile, a crowd from the streets is starting to gather and move inside the front doors of the church. The crowd includes local shopkeepers from nearby Front Street, natives, tourists, and especially the press.

The crowd also includes both Clive Lawson and Damian Rose.

As the government car sweeps around the church's circular driveway, Peter can't help thinking that the baby cathedral isn't a bad place for a sniper to come. Ugly deranged crowd; busy city streets; lots of Carnival confusion.

Stepping out of the official-looking Mercury, he hears the crowd's loud chant.

"United. State. Murderers!"

"United. State. Murderers!"

"Haile Selassie!"

"Haile Selassie!"

He watches a blur of black faces craning long necks, bulging veins, trying to find out what's going on all over their island.

It's so goddamn weird. A lot like Saigon in '73. It makes Peter feel like getting up with a microphone—explaining that most people in the U.S. are really okay. That they don't want all the island's bauxite—they don't want to hurt anybody, period.

Five men in dark suits and crisp white shirts meet him on the creaking front steps of the church. Brooks Campbell. Dr. Johnson. Harold Hill. The American ambassador himself . . .

A young Catholic priest takes Peter by the arm. Brief condolences and clumsy apologies are exchanged. Then the entourage quickly moves inside.

A TV news cameraman follows close behind them, stumbling along like a proud uncle at a wedding.

Two Marines follow with MAT submachine guns.

Meanwhile, Peter has put on his old baseball hat. Like Green Berets wearing their hats to funerals. Fuck your silly rules; conventions; fuck you!

"Not in here, Peter," the priest whispers. "The hat. Please."

Peter hears nothing but the sounds of two rows of plain wooden caskets. Lined up in front of the church's central altar, the boxes contain bodies still unclaimed after the Elizabeth's Fancy massacre. They hold the two dead agents from Mandeville Hospital. One of the temporary Red Cross caskets holds Jane.

"I know how you feel, Peter. You're only showing disrespect for Our Lord in this way."

"I doubt it means diddly-shit one way or the other to Our Lord. If it does, I don't buy his act either."

Finally, Father Brennan points at a particular casket to the right of the bright gold and red altar.

Peter stops in front of a casket with a place card: JANE FRANCES COOKE.

He looks down the line of U.S. Embassy and police officials. *Praying? Reciting the Pledge of Allegiance?* . . . The scene reminds him of the aftermath of some large tragedy he's seen in some news clip. Hundreds of bodies laid out in a grammar school cafeteria. Mourners rummaging through, searching for friends and relatives. Violated in their grief by television cameras.

"Aren't you going to open it?" he finally says to the priest. "I'd like to see her once more, please."

"We haven't been doing that," the priest says in a whisper. "These aren't the best conditions, Mr. Macdonald."

"I'd like to see her. I think we can all take it."

"Will you take off your hat?" the priest asks again. Peter takes off the baseball hat and the oblate consents to lift the cover for a brief viewing. It isn't what he thinks best—but the police chief says yes; the American ambassador says yes; and the young American man seems to know what he wants. . . .

With a loud, tearing noise, the cover comes off.

Peter looks down and sees a young-looking woman, only vaguely recognizable, surprisingly small now. . . . Jane has been prepared with what looks like an old lady's dusting powder and rouge. Her long blond curls seem brittle and stiff, like the wig on a child's doll. They haven't even used one of her own dresses. . . .

Oh, my God, no, Peter says over and over to himself. *Oh God Jesus. Goddammit. Goddammit.* If all those bastards hadn't been watching him, he would have let himself cry.

At the same time, Damian is watching the English killer high up in the church's choir loft. He's just three aisles behind Clive Lawson. No more than twelve feet away.

The expensive killer has had one opportunity, but he resisted it. Basically a good decision, Rose is thinking, calculating. This church is an interesting place for a shot, spectacular and unexpected—a thrill kill—but maybe it isn't the best place. *I would have done it here,* Damian thinks nonetheless. *Maybe on the way out . . .*

He studies Peter Macdonald standing in front of his girl-friend's coffin; he watches Brooks Campbell, Hill —ducks on a pond.

Soon, however, he sees Clive Lawson quietly leaving the choir loft; then the church altogether. The English killer has on a dark, contemporary rug that makes him look like many of the news reporters. Like the Secret Service men, for that matter. *Not bad for a traveling disguise.*

It appears that the grand finale, the *coup de grace,*

is going to have to wait just a little bit longer.

Damian leaves the Church of the Angels with the main body of the crowd.

He's an odd-looking sight with his baggy yellow trousers; his parasol; his jester's cap held respectfully in on hand.

Almost instantly he's accosted by a mob of kids wanting to play with Basil, the Children's Minstrel.

THURSDAY EVENING

All Thursday, San Dominica had been overturned and researched as desperately as it should have been the very night of the Elizabeth's Fancy massacre.

Owners of stores, cafés, taverns, private homes, were badgered by agents with the photokit drawing made from Peter's description.

Each and every motel, hotel, inn, chalet, hacienda, villa, lodge, casa, caravansary—black or white in clientele—was assaulted by marauding teams of local police and U.S. federal marshals. Rude Boys were hired to go out and mine for information in the larger city underworlds; among the cocaine and ganja dealers. Thousands of ordinary people were held up at the airports and boat docks—as well as at major roadblocks set all over the island.

Neither Damian Rose nor Clive Lawson turns up in any of the searches, however. Like a Martin Bormann, a Mengele—they're simply not the type of fish that winds up in a police dragnet.

The Season of the Machete

Bay of Pigs II is fast becoming Bay of Panic.

At 7:00 P.M. that night, a communications expert, Harvey Epstein, thinks that he's lucked into the first gold strike of the entire manhunt.

At the time of the discovery, Epstein is playing Canfield solitaire on the floor of a VW van. The van is parked about three hundred yards behind a large villa owned by the Charles Forlenza family (Sunasta Hotels) on San Dominica. Inside the van, Epstein is illegally bugging the Forlenza phones.

For two straight days now, the only thing he's heard is the Forlenza cook putting in her giggly orders for groceries at a place called the Coastown Gourmet Market. When the phone rings at seven, Harvey has a hunger attack.

He presses his earphones to one ear only, uncovers a club ace. Listens.

"Hello."

The first voice he records is a hood named Duane Nicholson. Nicholson is the man Isadore Goldman had brought with him to Government House on May 4.

Epstein assumes that the second voice is that of Damian Rose.

"I'm going to need those favors done for me," Rose says. "Put your part of things into operation."

"Tomorrow, right?" Nicholson asks.

Click. Buzz.

"Son of a bitch, Harvey! Son of a bitch!"

In less than an hour, Campbell and Harold Hill are listening to the tape in Coastown.

"Interesting." Campbell recognizes the silky voice. "It *is* Rose."

Still under guard at the Golf & Racquet Club, Peter sits in front of the San Dominican Broadcasting Corporation's blurry evening news.

For the first time in two days, he's clearheaded enough to consider the effect of a sniper's bullet. Every President's daydream . . . Your car windshield splatting against a bug. Half an ounce of steel entering your forehead at three thousand feet per second. Insane and nauseating.

Around 8:30, he makes a phone call to his family in Grand Rapids.

His mother can't understand why Air Force One hasn't flown him home already. "Make them put you on the first plane out of that place," Betsy Macdonald tells Peter. "My God, they've put you through enough already. They can come right up here to ask you any more questions they have. Tell them that, Peter. . . ."

Peter's father wants to know what the real story is. He's talked to his friend Senator Pflanzer, and Pflanzer wants to know too. "Pete, don't take any chances for those sorry bastards," Colonel Edward Macdonald says—Big Mac. "They're not doing shit for us any more—the whole damn government. They don't deserve anything back from us. I mean it."

As he listens, occasionally talks, Peter tries to picture Big Mac and Little Betsy. He sees them maybe ten years younger than they really are now. He sees the Super Six posing like some roughneck hockey team.

"I'll try to get home real soon," he says to his father. "Tell that to Mom. Tell my brothers too. Miss the hell out of all of you. I really do."

After the call, Peter just sits in the dark pseudo-tropics condominium bedroom.

Thinking.

He imagines a slow-motion pistol shot to a man's forehead. Like the famous Vietnamese execution photograph. The Tall Blond Man's head actually vaporizing.

At 1:30 in the morning, one of the CIA agents

comes into the bedroom—a little Italian guy who's always imitating Peter Falk.

"We're going to move you, Pete. Get ready, will you?"

Getting dressed, Peter prepares himself mentally. No point in getting scared now. Scared or stupid . . . Maybe there is, but fuck it.

Three agents with automatic rifles walk him to a station wagon waiting outside with the motor running.

A quick breath of fresh air. Appropriately fishy smell of the sea. No *ca-rack* of a rifle from the dark palm trees.

They ride to the Dorcas Hotel in Coastown in eerie silence. No questions asked; no information volunteered. No phony-baloney bullshit on their side or his.

The gray-haired CIA man—Harold Hill—is waiting for him inside the new hotel suite. A pleasant-enough place—like a Holiday Inn.

"My family has put in a formal complaint to the State Department." Peter lies simply and effectively. "It went through Senator Pflanzer," he announces to Hill and to Brooks Campbell, sitting in the living room.

"If you don't give me a crack at the blond mystery man, I'm going to force you to send me home. You know the tune—'War Hero Claims CIA Monkeyshines'!"

"All right, all right." The gray-haired man nods. A very sober, professor type, Peter notices. "Let's sit down and talk, Peter."

By 2:00 A.M., Peter Macdonald is officially part of the manhunt for Damian and Carrie Rose.

Shortly afterward, the fat black police chief arrives at the Dorcas. Strange man! Dr. Johnson just sits around talking with Peter. About the initial mistake by his constable at Turtle Bay; his own mistakes during the difficult case; about the night he'd spent with Jane at Mandeville Hospital.

"I couldn't sleep at home," the likable San Dominican finally says. "I thought you might understand."

"I understand." Peter smiles. "I think this is going to be an awfully long night too. Glad you're here, Doctor."

Damian had gotten uncharacteristically grubby—
vacant-eyed and distracted during the last months
of our preparation for San Dominica. His hair was
hardly ever combed. He spent entire days inside
the house, wandering in wrinkled silk pajamas. He
was obsessed with the idea of master criminals.
. . . I came home one night to find him reading a
book called *On Aggression,* babbling about brown
rats and piebald eagles. Another time he was
reading *The Rise and Fall of the Third Reich.* Lots
of Nazi books after that. The Master Criminal
Race, he called them . . .

The Rose Diary

Trelawney, San Dominica

In a small den lit by a black-and-white TV, Damian
sits cleaning an M-21 sniper's rifle. First he presses
out the rear pin and opens the rifle. Then he withdraws
the bolt and bolt carrier assembly. He withdraws the
thin firing pin retaining pin. Withdraws the cam pin,
the bolt from the bolt carrier.

On and off, he watches Alfred Hitchcock's *Notorious*
coming over the island's erratic TV network.

Overall, Damian decides, he could have been a
much better performer than the very one-dimensional

Cary Grant. He isn't certain if he could have been as good as a Claude Rains or an Ingrid Bergman, though. Those two were perfectionists. They could have made something out of Basil, the Children's Minstrel.

When the rifle's cleaned, when the M-21 is all back together, he goes into the bathroom, where he works for another hour or so.

Using a mixture of Quiet Touch and Miss Clairol, he dyes his hair what the package calls "blue-black," with gray highlights. Damian's own hair color.

Now there's only one tall blond Englishman: Clive Lawson.

And only one more day.

Before Damian Rose calls it a night, he takes a new field machete out of its cheesecloth wrapping. He lays the knife out carefully by his rifle.

Then the Tall Black-Haired American goes off to sleep.

Part III

The Perfect Ending

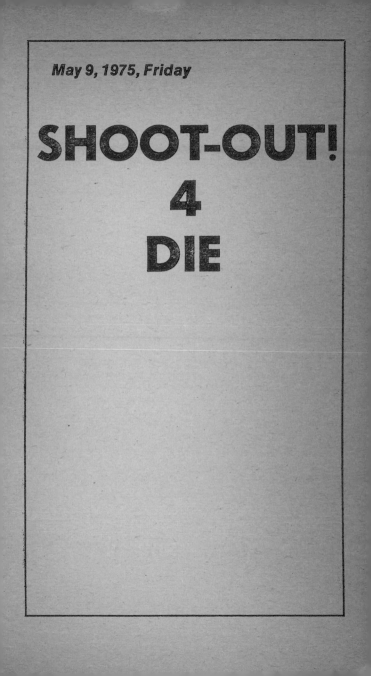

May 9, 1975, Friday

SHOOT-OUT!
4
DIE

May 9, 1975; Coastown, San Dominica

FRIDAY MORNING, THE LAST DAY
OF THE SEASON

Dr. Johnson breaks open a croissant, dabs half of the crisp roll with guava jelly, and watches Peter out of the corner of his eye.

"What a damn wonderful time for living it could have been." Peter shakes his head as he speaks to the fat black policeman.

The young American man is looking *especially* American in the bright light of morning. He's wearing a forest-green (holey, punky) SEE BEAR MOUNTAIN T-shirt; wrinkled athletic shorts; no shoes or socks; his ratty old baseball hat.

He's rubbing his bare feet together like sticks trying to make a fire.

"Swimming." He goes on with his spiel. "Sailing. Playing basketball, if you're a recidivist like me . . . Running around in a baseball cap like you're ten years old again and don't care . . . All kinds of wonderful, life-wasting crap. Nothing too serious, you know. R&R."

The middle-aged police chief is beginning to feel very tired, depressed. He keeps remembering the night he spent in the hospital with the blonde girl. Moreover, he's begun to feel paternal toward the young American. He likes Peter. *Sometimes he feels it's them against all the rest.*

"This island used to be that way. When I was a boy. I don't know if the world will let you do that any more. Be carefree."

Peter nods without saying anything.

He and the police chief are sitting under a striped yellow umbrella on a sixteenth-floor terrace of the Dorcas Hotel.

Across the terrace from them, two CIA men stand by the railing with their suit jackets off. With old-fashioned shoulder holsters strapped across their white shirts. Behind them, Coastown stretches out like a giant, glittering carnival. One story above, the roof of the Dorcas is yellow, the color of gold teeth. *The sloping roof is too steep for anyone to climb on,* someone who knows about such things has decided.

Peter throws his head back and looks around and around a cloudless, china-blue skyscape.

He starts to think about heroes, leaders, inspiration. . . . Once, when he was a plebe, he remembered going to a humanities symposium—"Is the Hero Dead in Western Civilization?" Four history and classics professors answered—shouted to the rafters—*Yes! Yes! Dead and buried!*

Well, dammit, people still needed heroes. He did, anyway . . . Ulysses, Churchill, Lincoln . . . whoever! Somebody! . . . That unbelievable ass Nixon. Gerry Ford. Jesus! Didn't they know anything about being leaders? Heroes? . . . If Kissinger could get to be a sex object, Richard Nixon could have at least gotten up to the level of human being.

"Man, oh, man, oh, man," he says in rhythm with

his neck and head circles. "It's so damn unbelievable, isn't it? Worse than Vietnam, and that really sucked. Bad, Meral, bad . . . I keep fantasizing that Janie is going to be alive again."

Trelawney, San Dominica

Damian Rose passes the first three hours of the morning struggling to fix a badly misused twenty-five-foot Bertram Sportsman.

Naked to the waist, dressed in striped cotton pants only, he works on the speedboat's trim-planes first; then replaces all the plugs; then does what he can about the engine's timing.

The Caribbean is a pretty dark blue in the early morning. The cove where he works is a Technicolor blur. Fuzzy blue and gold and white brilliance. Like movies shot through a Vaselined lens.

The cove is also neatly hidden from passing sea traffic; a little dogleg right behind a hill thick with palmettos.

Tucked up in the hills behind the cove is the home of a famous Caribbean landscape painter, an old recluse named Eric Downes. Hidden in a closet with stacks of bare canvases, Downes now lies dead.

As he tunes the boat's engine, Damian's mind slips back and forth between the Caribbean and France. Between the start of this working year, and the end of it . . . He remembers walks with Carrie through the Luxembourg Gardens; whole afternoons wasted in the Tuileries, the Place des Vosges, café-sitting around St.-Germain-des-Prés.

After he finishes the engine work, Rose takes an extra gas tank and two M-21 rifles down below into the cabin. He leaves the new field machete up in the cockpit.

When he finally looks at his watch, he's surprised to see that it's nearly nine. That means Carrie ought to be on her way to Morocco.

As he settles down to wait, Damian begins to whistle sweet "Lili Marlene." A truly great song. A tune that never fails to remind him of Carrie.

Zurich, Switzerland

Wearing a blue-gray shift and gray Valentino turban,
she sits across from a red-mustached, very fat Munchkin, S. O. Rogin, in the Schweizer Kreditverein in
Zurich.

Between the two of them, a soft leather Hermès
attaché case lies on a heavy marble table. Over their
heads, a crystal chandelier provides adequate light,
though filled with a blizzard of dust motes.

Rogin speaks English with a thick German-Swiss
accent; with one bushy eyebrow curiously arched.

"You wish to withdraw all six hundred twenty-nine
thousand?"

Carrie considers the question for a moment.

"Yes. All of it," she then says. Very businesslike.

"Very well, then. All right. How would you like
your money?"

The American woman takes out a blue pack of
cigarettes—Gauloises. The banker produces a klunky
silver lighter. As Rogin lights her cigarette, a strong
smell of kerosene wafts up. Then the lighter clicks
shut like an aspirin tin.

"What would you suggest?" Carrie asks.

The fat Munchkin begins to grin. "What would I suggest? For starters, I would suggest we transfer the funds directly to your new bank. *Tout de suite,* Mrs. Chaplin. Easy as apple pie. No suitcases."

"No. I'm afraid I must have the cash in hand, Herr Rogin."

"Hmmm. Of course." The red-haired man nods. "Will madame be needing a security guard, then? I will explain to you the simple procedure for—"

"I'll be fine." Carrie smiles, effectively cutting the man off. "If you read in *New Zurchen* about someone murdered in the streets downtown," she goes on, "you'll know that someone tried to take away my money."

The Munchkin—an American and British detective fan—laughs with genuine good humor.

"No one is ever murdered in Zurich, madame. Not in that manner, anyway." The banker laughs once again.

Then Rogin goes away to arrange for the six hundred twenty-nine thousand—one million five hundred thousand in Swiss francs.

As he walks through the elegant bank, S. O. Rogin wonders if the pretty lady is running away from her husband. He views Mrs. Chaplin as a sort of . . . Faye Dunaway type.

The fat man recalls Miss Dunaway in a scene from *Windmills of the Mind.* No, no. From *The Thomas Crown Affair.* A wonderful escapist movie.

All about robbing the banks of Boston.

Forty minutes later, Carrie Rose walks out of the Kreditverein with the Hermès briefcase full of Swiss francs. She's beginning to perspire now; her skin is prickling. She's paranoid about strangers on the Zurich streets.

The tall, long-haired American woman goes just

one block across the Stampfenbachstrasse, however. She enters the impressive Union Bank of Switzerland, and redeposits the cash.

All part of the master plan.

Sooner or later, we were certain they would throw
Macdonald to us. Harold Hill was an executive:
good executives are executors. Predictable because they try to be so logical . . . Damian never
tries to figure out the mazes, just the mice. . . .
The Rose Diary

Wahoo Cay, San Dominica

FRIDAY AFTERNOON

At two in the hot, hot of the afternoon, Damian
floats over an exquisite range of shallow barrier reefs.

Sunbathing in the twenty-five-foot Sportsman, watching mullets and snipe eels forage and dart through
the bottle-green waters, he's beginning to let his mind
drift to thoughts of meeting Carrie. Seedy Morocco.
Casbahs. A perfect ending for this crime. The two who
get away with it.

Damian is convinced that San Dominica represents
the best free-lance work done since John Kennedy was
hit in Dallas. He knows it.

Just a few more hours to go now. All of it heading
helter-skelter yet inevitably toward a small pinprick
in time and space.

Actually, the end begins in a most understated manner; a curious contrast to everything that's gone before it.

At 3:15, Dr. Meral Johnson and Brooks Campbell escort Peter down out of the Dorcas Hotel.

The young American man is wearing gray cotton pants with a loose-fitting gray zipper jacket. Underneath the jacket is a Walther PPK revolver. A neat, tough gun. Compliments of Great Western Air Transport, of Harold Hill in particular.

The three men get into a white Dodge Charger idling in the hotel carport. Campbell looks around for rooftop snipers, and that seems almost funny to Peter. "Uh, that's *our* fort," he finally has to say.

From the hotel, they drive to a secluded villa owned by the Charles Forlenza family. A big flamingo-pink Hollywood-style house.

Both Campbell and Harold Hill have hopes now that the man staying at the villa—Duane Nicholson—will either contact, or be contacted by, Damian Rose. They've put a five-car stakeout team on the house.

Officially, Peter is along to make any necessary identification. Officially, he doesn't have a gun. Unofficially, Harold Hill is beginning to troll bait for Rose.

In some ways, he too is reminded of November in 1963. Very messy stuff. A marvel how you can smooth out these things in the end—*national security matters.*

At six o'clock in Washington, a Mrs. C. Rose checks into the St. James Hotel. Some mail is waiting for her —letters from Damian. Very mushy and adolescent, Port-Smithe thinks.

At seven o'clock in Zurich, Carrie waits in her hotel suite. She watches swans glide over the lake of Zurich, makes casual notes for the diary, tries to take care of all the final details the way Damian would. . . .

At a quarter to eight, a chip of burnt-orange sun sinks without a trace behind the Forlenza villa.

His heart starting to thump out strange warnings, Peter watches Isadore Goldman's expensive lackey walk outside the big stucco house. He considers that *Isadore Goldman* is just a name to him; considers that he really doesn't want to die. He wants to shoot the tall blond mercenary somehow; wants to go home to Michigan again. Like thriller-chiller novel endings.

"Blue. This is White Flag," Brooks Campbell whispers into the car's crackling shortwave radio. "You guys all awake?"

"Peter?" Meral Johnson winks into the car's rearview mirror. "Awake?"

"He's just going out for a roast beef on rye," Peter says, feels electricity anyway. "I'm wide awake, Meral." Peter grins at the fat policeman. Neither of them talks to Campbell.

Easygoing and, to Peter's eye, unconcerned, Duane Nicholson shuffles across the villa's front lawn in Indian moccasins, casual slacks, some sort of sky-blue surfer's shirt. A very expendable type, Peter can't help thinking. The kind of guy who always gets shot first in adventure movies . . . Having walked the length of the house, the curly-headed hood disappears into a dark three-car garage.

Minutes later, a dull-white Stingray rolls out onto the driveway.

Low-slung in the driver's seat, resting comfortably behind a stained-pigskin steering wheel, the Las Vegas mobster wheels the powerful car out to the dirt access road. Then, bolting and roaring like an animal that isn't used to restraints, the Corvette chugs down toward the Shore Highway.

The Season of the Machete

Izzie Goldman's man is heading into Coastown.

Sitting in the back seat of one of five surveillance cars, Peter has already clicked his mind into combat readiness. Just in case. He figures the punk hoodlum is going to dinner, though. Everyone in the surveillance cars figures the same thing.

Tryall, San Dominica

A shadowy figure thrusts itself up a long sliver of dock due west of Coastown's twinkling pocket of electric lights.

To the running man's back, dark tuna boats lie on the horizon of the Caribbean. Beyond the fishing boats are several thousand miles of open sea. Then, the southern extremes of Europe.

For his last night on San Dominica, Damian Rose has chosen a beige security guard's uniform. Pitch black is smeared on his face and hands so that from a distance he looks like a native.

An M-21 with a complicated-looking sight is slung over his left shoulder; a heavy sugar-cane machete is tied to his waist.

Looking both ways and back over his shoulder first, he starts across a wide field toward a distant, narrow road.

Peter glances at his watch: 8:35.

The Chevrolet Corvette and three surveillance cars are creeping slowly down Charles Henry Street on the northern outskirts of Coastown.

The cars slink up a crowded side avenue with old wrecks of American autos lined along both sides.

Black children in colorful rags dart in and out of the parked cars. Slouch-hatted Rude Boys whack the hoods of the passing night traffic.

The dusty Corvette sweeps up a dark, crowded lane that loops around then runs alongside Queen Anne's Park. The park is still jam-packed with laughing, running blacks practicing for Labor Day Carnival, the official end of the tourist season.

"He's on to us," Brooks Campbell whispers inside the white Charger. "What the fuck is that bastard doing?"

On the side of a damp, grassy hill, Damian Rose waits calmly with his M-21 and machete.

Not sixty yards away, completely unaware of Rose, Clive Lawson stands with an Uzi submachine gun resting on his hips. He too waits.

In the back seat of the Charger, Peter is absorbing flashing pieces of Queen Anne's Park. Nearly subliminal stuff. Men and boys in flowing white shirts. Dancing bonfires. A few purplish clouds moving fast in a high wind . . . It's a little like being on patrol—a strange, worthless night patrol dreamed up by the usual morons. *Shoot anyone who doesn't answer to the name Carl Yastrzemski.*

"He's leading us to the tall blond man." Peter answers Campbell's earlier question. "He's doing exactly what you wanted him to do. . . . All we have to do is figure out why."

Just then, the Corvette swings wide around a big City of Coastown truck. The Corvette takes an impossibly sharp, skidding left—then the low-slung car starts to accelerate up a hill as if it were flat ground.

"Brace yourselves, gentlemen," Meral Johnson yells out.

The steep hill comes and goes—then sweeps down roller-coaster style on quiet, narrow side streets.

An unofficial Grand Prix race is beginning. People along the sidewalks are starting to scream at the fast-moving, souped-up cars.

Eight-thirty-nine. Damian checks the M-21 carefully. Checks the ammo. Clive Lawson still has the submachine gun on his hip.

His stomach floating up in his chest cavity, his heart pounding like a tight bass drum, Peter watches Isadore Goldman's man shoot down a narrow, unmarked driveway.

"White Flag" nearly misses it.

A green Mazda misses, spins off into berry bushes. Harold Hill's blue Cougar makes the hair turn in the middle of the road.

Another quick right turn follows in unfair progression. An immediate, impossible left. Then a frighteningly straight, four-block-long speedway appears out of nowhere. One catch: the speedway is blanketed with people.

From the bouncing rear seat, Peter watches a blur of panicked, running blacks. They'd been loitering around the streets, catching a cool breeze. . . . Now they're diving onto the dirt sidewalks. A few crazy ones seem to be imitating toreadors, flapping shirts and sweaters at the passing, weaving cars. A woman is hit—*bang*.

Eight-forty-three.

Inside the white Charger, Brooks Campbell unholsters his revolver. Dr. Johnson is sitting on the car horn—creating one sustained scream. All the car horns are screaming.

The Corvette twitches into third. Then up into fourth gear.

Peter takes his gun out of his shoulder holster. PPK Walther. Tough gun.

The low-slung sportscar opens up nearly a two-block lead on the others. It's getting small fast. A white box and flashing taillights—hugging the road—leaving the city like a ground rocket.

Then Brooks Campbell is screaming, pointing at the Corvette, which is suddenly way over on the right.

The Corvette is jetting down a dark country road. Opening up a quarter-mile lead.

Clive Lawson is getting the Uzi ready now. He plants his feet in the soft dirt of the hillside. He stretches his arms, right first, then left.

"We're losing him, goddammit. We're losing him!"

The fat, sweating police chief twirls the steering wheel.

The white Charger spins. Turns. Just misses turning over. Peter is thrown across the back seat. Feels his head crack against a side window.

They're accelerating down the dark back road with the Corvette completely out of sight now. Brooks Campbell radioing for reinforcements, armies. Asking where the Tryall Road comes out . . .

Eight-forty-four. Damian braces the M-21 against a coconut palm. Watches through his night scope.

Then all of the surveillance cars brake suddenly for a fork around a huge, spreading kapok tree.

"Left! Hill will go . . ."

The last part of Brooks Campbell's instruction is drowned out.

Peter is screaming at Meral Johnson to step on the gas.

Unbelievably, the Dodge Charger's side front window disintegrates.

A loud, high-powered rifle is exploding over and over in the dark woods. Methodical sniping. A professional marksman.

The Charger's roof explodes. Another window blows up. The car's trunk takes a blast that would have killed an elephant.

Meral Johnson is screaming for Macdonald to stay down.

Somebody's head slams against a window and breaks right through it.

"On the floor! On the floor!"

The roof is hit again. Another blast hits somewhere in the greenhouse—the window-frame area. Gun blasts pound the car like sledge hammers.

At least twenty explosions come within thirty seconds.

Then the quiet of the dark back road is back. A magic silence. Millions of twitting bugs. Tropical birds. The transition back and forth almost incomprehensible.

The wounded Charger is still rolling. Its tires are making pathetic little clicking noises.

Meral Johnson has his hand down on the floor in the front seat. Flat down on the gritty brake pedal. Finally, he stops the Charger.

Men from "Green Flag" are running to help. Bouncing sunglasses. Wingtips slapping on macadam.

Harold Hill is running from way down the road. Screaming something. Looking like the father of a drowning child.

"Macdonald!" the black policeman suddenly screams himself. "Macdonald!"

A low groan comes from inside the car.

Peter sits up in the back seat. Starts to shake off

glass. *Gash in his head,* he realizes. *Blood . . . shit . . .*

He sees Campbell up in front. Looking at the shattered windshield as if he's finally solved the whole goddamn awful thing.

Except that the Great Western Air Transport man is too dead to solve things any more.

A revolutionary, American-made bullet has pierced one side of the handsome face, tumbled over once, tried to tumble over again—exploded brain matter all over the walls and roof of the man's skull. Like a bulldozer trying to crowd into a living room.

And then Peter isn't looking at Campbell any more. He's running. For the first time since April 30—Turtle Bay—he's moving like a certifiable madman, holding the Walther automatic like a baton in a relay race.

He's seen the Tall Blond Man up in the woods.

Damian scrutinizes Harold Hill and the black police chief in the steaming headlights of the unmarked police cars.

Then Rose retreats farther back into the thick brush and brambles. Back closer to the boat. Escape. Carrie.

Just one more scenario now.

As he pushes his way through dark tree shapes and hanging moss, Peter hears shrieking birds and bugs all around him.

The moon seems to be racing through the shiny leaf ceiling over his head.

After about seventy yards of the restrictive bushes, he emerges into the wide-open space of the Tryall Club's golf course.

He can see the Caribbean then, a faint line of foamy surf. He can make out the main clubhouse, a long, low building with half a hundred windows facing the golf course—*closed for the Summer Season.*

No tall Blond Man. And one burning question: *why hadn't the rifleman gotten him?*

Peter's wide eyes methodically search the dark Tryall golf course. He's in a combat trance now. All his movements automatic: search and destroy; kill the mercenary, or get killed.

His eyes run over the neat, handsome clubhouse; along the dark, flagstone patio and walkway; past hedges, gardens; down a long, rocking-chair porch.

Somewhere between the bramble and the clubhouse he'd missed a turn by the tall, running man. His powers as a tracker of men are rusty, Peter realizes—gone altogether, kaput. A good Vietnamese would have killed him by now.

A stitch of white lightning lights up the night sky.

Then Peter hears Meral Johnson's first scream.

Usually more athletic, he takes a clumsy header onto the flat, rolling lawns.

Not very expert, he realizes as he hits down hard. More like a heavy box bouncing out the back of a speeding truck.

Except that when he stops bouncing, he's still alive. *Chewing dirt,* as Sergeant P. Macdonald once instructed new men in the field.

And Johnson is still screaming like an agonized madman.

"Stay down, Macdonald! Stay there! . . . Stay there, Peter!"

Up near the clubhouse, Peter spots the shadow of a man with a rifle.

The blond man? One of Hill's people? Too dark to be sure.

His heart starts to pound so hard he can't catch his breath. His mind fills with choking rage. *He wants the bastard so badly! It's fucked-up, pathetic as hell— it's against everything he's been trying to make of himself since Vietnam. But he wants the man all the same. He wants him so badly it aches. Infinite pain . . . Why didn't you shoot me, you prick?*

271

Suddenly, automatic rifle fire comes out of a grove of trees to his right. Rifles winking in the night. Licks of orange flame.

As he looks on, bullets mercilessly rip and pound the fancy clubhouse. Expensive windows crumble out of the dining room. Lights break all over. A drain pipe is blown off a wall like *papier-mâché*.

Peter carefully aims the Walther at the shadowy man. He gets to squeeze off a single wild shot. A long, impossible shot that comes surprisingly close. Then the shadow with the rifle is gone. All the shooting stops and it starts to rain.

"FUCK YOU!" Peter stands up in the rain and shouts.

"FUCK YOU!

"FUCK YOU, YOU LOUSY SON OF A BITCH!"

Slanting sheets of rain came in cool, steamy torrents
—making it nearly impossible to see. Like having a
gunfight in a steam bath. Total confusion.

Somehow or other, he's thinking, Clive Lawson—
late guttersnipe out of Billingsgate, late of the British
Commandos, late of the unannounced Third World
wars—has gotten himself into a nasty booby
trap. . . .

There'd been no word around that Damian and
Carrie Rose were double-dealers. Quite the opposite,
in fact . . . Christ! Why hadn't he stayed in Miami!
Lived to fight another day?

The mercenary lies sideways in a stonework gutter,
like a hurt fish. He gropes around for a flesh wound
and finds his left side to be numb. Then it burns as if
he's set a gasoline torch to himself.

Lawson turns his left arm to his face, Looks at the
glowing silver dials on his watch: 9:12. Too bloody
bad. His escape had been arranged for nine. Right
after he gunned down Campbell. The Roses were supposed to get him out of there. Supposed to.

He starts to crawl on his belly inside the littered

gutter. He makes little fish-fin strokes with his hands. Then, at the end of the gutter, Clive Lawson gets up and starts to run.

Damian is God—slowly counting off the final few seconds of confusion.

He studies the teeming grounds through a light intensifier mounted on the stock of his sniper's rifle. The sighting device lets him see in the dark. It throws whatever is in the rifle scope into a clear circle of eerie, Christmas-green light.

Watching the human vignettes in the strange green light, he slides his index finger gently down onto the rifle trigger. His finger takes in the slack of the trigger. . . .

Peter's face is so wet it's a bitch just to stop his eyes from blinking.

Rain water is rushing off his forehead. Rolling off his nose. He's actually choking on the rain. Getting frightened now because he can't see.

There's no sound around him except for the downpour, and his own heavy breathing. His mind is racing at a madhouse pace. Throwing out Technicolor combat images, fire-fight scenes, disconnected phrases.

Up ahead he can see the outline of overturned furniture on a dining veranda. Wrought-iron tables and chairs. Broken plant and flower pots.

He takes one more step forward. . . .

Then Peter sees the shape of another man across the open-air patio.

The man is crouching in front of baby palm trees. So far, he doesn't realize that someone's on the terrace with him.

Peter uses the cover of the loud rain to circle around closer. Inch by inch he gets ten feet closer. Fifteen feet . . . Another ten feet and he thinks he'll have a decent pistol shot.

He cons his mind into thinking that he can't miss, not even in the rain. He'll squeeze off at least two quick shots, he knows. Then as many more shots as he can get in. Hopefully, the man will never get to use his Uzi.

Then the tall man actually begins to move closer to him.

He's moving sideways in a crouch, and he still has his back to Peter. He's moving like a professional Army man.

Peter wipes the back of his hand across his eyes. The rain water makes them sting like hell. Now he can see that the man's hair is blond.

There is no way I can miss hitting this man, he reminds himself. *Zen marksmanship. It's like standing twenty paces away from one of those big overturned dining tables. Taking your damn good time for a shot. Seeing not whether or not you'll hit it, but how close you can come to the little hole in the center for the table's umbrella.*

How close he can come to the axis of the tall blond man's spine.

Kneeling on one knee, arms out stiff, perfectly straight, two hands on the Walther, Peter carefully gets the blond man in his sight.

He brings an image of the first machete murder into his mind. Then Jane—Jane on the beach at Horseshoe Bay, the shrunken body in the cathedral.

He looks straight down the black barrel into the man's back. Then Peter finally speaks to the tall blond man.

"Hey!" he says. "Do you remember me, mister? Hey, shithead!"

Inside the Tryall clubhouse, a nervous police constable lights a stick match.

As he strikes match after match, the policeman desperately tries to figure out a row of master switches inside a steel-gray cabinet.

He considers the switches until his last match burns down, then he decides to give Number 1 a try. He flicks the black switch and the lights in the small room he's in come on bright and scary. Then the constable can see two distinct rows in the control box: Numbers 1 through 6, and 7 through 12.

His shaking hand moves quickly down the first row.

As the man on the dining veranda pivots around to face Peter, every light in this magnificently frightening world seems to come on all at once. Night lights blink on down the first fairway. A tape system on the veranda starts to play soft dinner music.

Then loud thunder seems to originate on the back patio of the Tryall clubhouse. Sparks of gunfire light up all over the lawns.

Damian Rose is firing his M-21. Harold Hill shoots an expensive Italian-made rifle. The entire force surrounding the Tryall clubhouse is blasting away at the suddenly bright, white building.

Peter's first shot hits the blond man—a dark hole opens on his forehead; then Peter is hit so hard he can't believe it. It feels as if he's been blind-sided by a three-thousand-pound automobile. Hit deliberately. So fucking sad. So sad . . .

Windows are breaking everywhere. The wrought-iron furniture is ringing out pings and pangs. Wood thuds hard as it catches errant rifle shots.

A singularly loud crack echoes and a speck of the dead Englishman's head flies off.

The fallen Englishman is hit again on the side of his face.

A third rifle shot enters the back of his head as he lies face down on the flagstone patio.

Then it's all blinding light and rain. Clean rain that appears slightly blue in the white light. It's all soothing, steady rain noise with no gunshots at all.

Men stream across the flat, muddy lawns. . . . Gray suits soaked to darker colors. Short pants and pillbox hats. Submachine guns and pistols and dark rifles swinging loose on leather straps.

The rain is shining like expensive jewelry in all the trees. There's an eerie quiet now.

Harold Hill is walking straight ahead, looking ridiculous, as if he were lost in the rain. His Topsiders slap down on the patio near Peter Macdonald's head, then he turns away.

Peter feels himself getting sick, and he fights the nauseous feeling with everything he has left.

A circle of curious faces begins to form over him— like being on an operating table, like being a heart-attack victim on a New York City street. . . . Black soldiers and FBI and CIA men. All smiling as if they're his old best friends. Congratulating him as if he's scored the winning touchdown.

The black police chief is bent over him, trying to show him where he's been hit. *The stomach? The rib cage?* Goddamn nice bastard, Peter thinks. "I'm okay." He grins at the black man.

And in the middle of all the confusion—the blinding lights, rain, police sirens, an ambulance driving up on the lawns—a bearded white man in a suit is dragging a corpse by its hair. Some bearded CIA prick.

A creepy black policeman is snapping flash-bulb photos. Spread-eagle shots of the body that's being dragged. Shots of Peter being cradled in Meral Johnson's arms.

An American man is working with a buzzing electric camera that takes pictures in the dark.

Suddenly they bring the body to Peter and everybody's trying to talk to him all at one time. Peter sits up and waves them away.

He stares down at bloodshot eyes turned up as far as they'll go in their sockets. Eyes caught in terrible shock and surprise.

No wonder, though, Peter thinks. The right side of the head looks as if it's been bitten into. There's no nose to speak of; what's left of the mouth is frozen in a smirky death cry.

Peter flashes back to Turtle Bay—*the tall, haughty man. Fifteen seconds* . . .

He concentrates on the blown-up face. Wet blond hair, slicked down flat by the rain. Long, athletic body.

He feels very tired now, mind fighting against big, strong waves of ugly shit. . . . *Dr. Johnson saying something to him* . . . But all he feels like doing is shouting at the dead man.

"He's the one," he finally whispers to the black police chief. "He's the one, goddamn him to hell."

Which is about the time Peter finally hears what Meral Johnson is saying to him.

Running in a low, infantry crouch, Damian's trooper boots squish across a slippery wooden ramp at the Tryall Club's yacht basin. He climbs movable stairs down onto the floating dock, steps into the lurching Bertram Sportsman, and begins to smile in spite of himself.

Then he begins to laugh. A chilly, unnatural laugh.

He can barely distinguish voices in the distant, babbling commotion coming from up around the main clubhouse. He sees the thousand-watt floodlights flashing through swaying palm and banana trees up and down the first fairway.

Then the bouncing red lights of two ambulances turn a corner of the clubhouse building. Siren screams cut through the rain and wind like sharp knives.

Finally, after more than a year, after the most insanely exhausting ordeal he's ever put himself through, it's over and done with.

Up on the Tryall Club's veranda, the ex-Green Beret, All-American Boy, unimpeachable witness, has identified Clive Lawson as the Tall Blond Man from

Turtle Bay. . . . The English killer's hair, his hair style, height, facial features, are nearly identical with the man Macdonald had seen April 30. At a quick glance, Rose and Lawson are look-alikes—and a glance was all Peter had ever had. Fifteen seconds on a bicycle.

Moreover, the way Lawson's face wound up, it's academic anyway.

The Great Damian Rose is officially dead. Killed on his most audacious, tympanic contract. The psychological logic of the ploy is classic. Hubris strikes again. Precisely the end they all would have predicted for him. Like Evel Knievel dying on a motorcycle.

Now, if Carrie succeeds in Washington, they're home free. No one will come looking for the Roses for quite some time. Maybe not ever.

Another smile drifts over Damian's thin, pretty lips. The pure satisfaction of playing the game well. The absolute, spine-tingling beauty of it. Like having built one's own cathedral in this slapdash age.

Moving quickly but quietly, Rose starts the blowers, then unties the Dacron stern line that holds the Sportsman to San Dominica. The twenty-five-foot speedboat is shaking like mere flotsam in the unsteady sea; the rain continues to teem.

As he unloops a final knot in the bowline, a man appears in the hatchway coming from the sleeping cabin below.

The man is tall and thin, dressed in a gray slicker with hood. He throws back the hood and his silver-gray hair completes the perfect yacht-clubber image.

"Hello, there," the dark figure says. "My name is Harold Hill. I thought we should meet."

The director of Great Western Air Transport hoists himself into the stormy cockpit. *Harry the Hack. Dependable Harry.*

"Actually, you do nice work." He continues to speak as he climbs up top. "Stay put, now. Don't get up on my account. Don't move a fucking muscle."

Pointing a dark Walther at the younger man's heart, Hill rests his bottom on the back of a swivel chair.

"Hair dyed a nice shade of black." He shows his teeth in an appreciative smile. "Cut to look like some Goober from Lithuania. That's nice. What did you plan to do from here?"

Damian tries to keep himself calm. Icy. *Think straight lines. Think nothing but straight lines.* As he speaks, his mind races back and forth through his alternatives; through all the possibilities for this situation.

"I was going to take a commercial flight off the island." He speaks softly. At the same time, he's thinking that something about Harold Hill is bothering him; he can't put his finger on it exactly. "Now that I'm officially dead, you know."

"Macdonald isn't, you know," Harold Hill says. "I'm curious—why didn't you kill Macdonald too? The famous last shoot-out scenario?"

"I thought a live witness would be more convincing in the long run. Don't you think? . . . Macdonald was part of all this from the start, you know."

Hill seems a bit confused. "Macdonald was working for you? . . ."

Don't laugh at him, Damian thinks. *Don't laugh in his face. . . .*

"No. No . . . But right from the beginning we knew we'd need a witness to identify Lawson. To make our escape work right . . . We knew that Peter Macdonald rode around Turtle Bay every afternoon. So we planned a murder right there. *C'est ça.* Macdonald saw me because he was meant to see me. We even went to great lengths to strengthen his credibility afterward. . . . Tell me something. Did Carrie do this?"

Harold Hill shakes his head from side to side. "*I* ask the questions." He smiles.

The CIA director motions for the younger man to get up. Slowly.

As he stands, Hill knocks Rose back down with a gun-butt blow to the cheek. A vicious hit.

"Best I can do right now," Hill says through clenched teeth. "For Carole. My wife . . . Get up now. I won't hit you any more. I have lots of questions before I kill you, Rose. I have an interesting idea for that too."

His mouth all bloody, Damian gets up again. He holds his hands high, plain in sight. Like a magician about to do a trick.

At Hill's direction, Rose takes hold of the ladder going up to the dock.

"On our way across the lawn"—Damian speaks in calm, measured tones—"I want you to listen carefully to what I have to offer you. We can renew our partnership."

As the tall dark-haired man puts both hands on the metal ladder, the right side of his head explodes.

His face crashes forward against the aluminum slats. His chin bounces down two rungs, then he falls over backwards into the boat.

Harold Hill looks up to find the black police chief standing on the wooden ramp. Beside him is Macdonald, slightly bent over, holding a Walther pointed down at the boat.

"We followed you," Meral Johnson says simply. Peter says nothing.

As Hill starts to climb past the dead or dying man, he sees the sugar-cane machete lying across a leather seat. The most obscene murder weapon. The cleaver they'd used on Carole in Virginia.

In one unbelievable stroke, he brings it down powerfully across Rose's face. The hacking blow makes a noise like a butcher's cleaver. Damian snorts like a horse.

The field machete comes down again. A clumsy guillotine.

Finally, Hill kicks the head and it sloshes up against a sideboard. Floats in a dark pool of rain water.

Then Harold Hill climbs up the movable ladder.

He says nothing to the black policeman; nothing to Peter.

"What partnership was that?" Peter says. . . . Then he lets it go. . . . *Lets the sentence drown in the night air . . . It doesn't matter. Of course the CIA was in on it. . . .*

For a long moment they all stand on the wet ramp. The black and the young white man close together. None of them speaking. . . . Then Hill unties the last restraining rope. It doesn't end, the CIA man is thinking. Now these two have to be taken care of. . . .

As the Sportsman slowly drifts away, Meral Johnson fires several shots into the boat's bottom and sides.

"Let the fish have him," the black man says.

At first, Harold Hill's hands are trembling. Then, very slowly, the director begins to feel rather good. . . . In a way, he supposes, he's the hero of it all: the man who saved Central Intelligence.

Or maybe it's Carrie Rose who's the hero.

After all, it was Carrie who'd phoned the Embassy to tell him how to get Damian; who'd revealed the last details of the monster plot. . . . He should have told Rose that, Hill thinks too late. He should have told Damian that, in the end, Carrie had turned on him and set him up. *How very fucking pathetic. The woman he'd slept with for nine years, loved, presumably. His protégée, among other things . . . Well, she was going to get hers too. . . . A perfect ending.*

For a long time the three men stand in the rain,

watching the speedboat drift away. Listening to the gulps of the bobbing, sinking boat.

"Peter asked you a question before," Meral Johnson says. "What kind of partnership did you have with him?"

Suddenly, Peter raises the Walther again. *Sideways.* Almost without looking, it seems. The force of the single pistol shot knocks Hill ten feet out onto the water.

"Let the fish have both of them," Peter says.

He and the short, fat policeman slowly walk back to the clubhouse.

May 10, 1975, Saturday

RAID
ST. JAMES

May 10, 1975; Washington, D.C.

SATURDAY MORNING

At quarter past six on the morning of the tenth, two heavyweights from Langley—twenty-seven-year-old Alex Fletcher and Deputy John Devereaux—step out of a white Pontiac Lemans, then run across the dewy back lawns of the sedate, prohibitively expensive St. James Hotel.

Inside the fancy hotel, some of America's richer and more noted personages are fast asleep on the already pretty, blue-skied, spring morning.

Outside on the manicured back lawns, blackbirds are just beginning to make their little peeps and tu-witts. One hale fellow disappears over the garden fence as if he's going out to fetch the morning's *Post*.

Alex Fletcher is wearing a film director's bush jacket, brushed corduroys, with a Smith & Wesson .38 strapped across a cotton work shirt.

Devereaux, fifty-six years old, wears a dark suit with an open-necked white shirt. A cigarette hangs from his lower lip like a piece of white tape.

The two men sneak inside a gray metal door rarely used by anyone but St. James maintenance men.

Behind the door, they find a security guard asleep with a white Siamese on his belly. The man has passed out in a folding beach chair, snoring like broken-down machinery.

"Good morning." Devereaux grins. "Monsieur Le Chat."

"Some fucking joint," Fletcher whispers. "No wonder the D. C. police have such a big, throbbing dick of a job."

The two men proceed up battleship-gray back stairs; uncarpeted and unexpectedly dreary. A smelly cat litter sits on one stairwell.

They come out into an elegant hallway marked with a big pink five on powder-blue walls.

Fletcher whistles under his breath. "Now this is more like it."

The young agent taps a real crystal chandelier with his fingernail. "Class, Devereaux, class."

"I'll buy it for you and your girl friend," John Devereaux growls. "Right after we finish our business here. Present arms!"

The two men stop in front of Room 502. Big gold numbers on the softest powder blue. Tasteful molding. Escarping.

Alex Fletcher takes a deep breath, whispers a cynical ejaculation, then he slowly slides a hotel passkey into the lock.

The deputy brings a .44 Magnum out from under his sports jacket, a loud, dangerous cannon young Fletcher disapproves of entirely. "Nuclear Warfare," he's nicknamed the long black pistol.

He gives Devereaux a funny little smile. "Try not to blow me up by mistake. Just a passing thought. Ready?"

"For Harold Hill and Carole."

"Mmm."

The elaborate door swings over thick mauve carpeting.

The two agents look in on a light-haired woman sitting up in a rumpled double bed. A big room full of morning sun.

"Who are you?" the long-haired woman says. She reaches toward her night table.

"No!" Fletcher screams—the absolute top volume of his voice.

Then Devereaux's .44 detonates in the doorway.

The astonished woman literally flies against the red-velvet wall, the brass headrails of her bed. She gives out one small groan and her green eyes roll back. Then Betsy Port-Smithe slowly slides down to the floor.

Young Fletcher frowns and shakes his head. "No questions. No answers." The ambitious agent kicks over an end table. "Shit. Shit, Devereaux."

Devereaux shrugs. He sniffs the air. A funny combination of Joy perfume and smoky cordite.

The deputy throws open a window on Rock Creek Park, then stands there going through the woman's suede pocketbook. Inside, he finds letters from a man named Damian; he finds cards and papers that identify Carrie Rose. . . . Inside the night-table drawer, he finds a small .38 revolver.

"Better call them." Devereaux smiles. "Tell them they can stop worrying about this shitty bastard Mrs. Rose. No scandals in the White House for today."

Like Harold Hill, fifty-six-year-old John Devereaux is thinking that he's a hero too. They'd told him not to bring her back alive.

The Season of the Machete is finally over.

The Epilogue

The Summer Season

I am Superwoman . . . SuperRat . . . Superscuz.
. . . Damian trained me so that I was capable of
anything—then he let me do nothing. Stagnate.
He would have never even let me sell my diary.
When his own obsessions became impossible—a
liability to both of us—I had to kill him. No choice
in the matter. *Had to* . . . Now I'm all alone at the
top of the heap. The first Public Enemy on the
loose in decades . . . My prices start at $1,000,000
and I'm worth it. I'm like a Paris original, a one-of-
a-kind operation. Hiring me is like being able to
hire Manson, Speck, Himmler, Bormann. . . . I'll
do anything you can think of, and I'll think of
things you wouldn't. The Season of the Machete
was a preamble—as primitive as its name. It was
just a beginning. The Tool Age of violence and
disruption . . . Now comes the interesting part.
We're just entering the Machine Age, I believe.

The Rose Diary

June 13, 1975; Coastown, San Dominica

Feeling like a national hero, Prime Minister Joseph
Walthey parades through large, enthusiastic crowds in
Coastown's Horseshoe Beach District.

Paid admirers—civil servants, especially—circle him

like birds. They pat his cream suede suit jacket, reach out for his curly, slicked-down hair, reach to touch his round, black Santa Claus face.

Thirty-five-millimeter news footage is shot for special release to San Dominica's thirteen movie theaters. Hundreds of publicity photographs are taken for the world's newspapers.

At a high, colorful dais built over the boardwalk, over the shimmering Caribbean, Walthey announces that an era of new prosperity is dawning for San Dominica. The smiling, affable prime minister doesn't elaborate, however.

July 14, 1975; Coastown, San Dominica

In a special session of the San Dominican Assembly, Prime Minister Joseph Walthey is named president for life on the island. He makes a long speech about nationalism, the economy, and tourism on San Dominica: he lies at length.

October 1, 1975; Turtle Bay, San Dominica

The first casino to open on San Dominica is in the Playboy Club—not five miles from the Plantation Inn.

The grand opening is marred by minor student demonstrations.

Black boys and girls wave a psychedelic poster of Dassie Dredth that is making the rounds at the University of the West Indies and other schools throughout Central and South America. They play loud reggae and soul music, and some cars and walls at the Playboy are spray-painted DRED! The students wave signs that say JOE IS THE BLACK HITLER.

March 3, 1976; Zurich, Switzerland

Nearly ten months after Damian's death, on the afternoon of March 3, 1976, 4,500,000 Swiss francs are deposited in the numbered account of Mrs. Susan Chaplin in the Schweizer Kreditverein in Zurich. The money represents nearly $2,000,000 from the diary sale.

Curiously, three days after her withdrawal of 600,-000 American dollars in May of 1975 (a Damian-style safeguard—what if he had eluded Hill at the Tryall Club?), the woman had redeposited her money in a new account.

Filling out the necessary tax forms for the 1976 deposit, S. O. Rogin finds himself thinking of Mrs. Chaplin in terms of the actress Faye Dunaway once again. So many actors and actresses, the red-faced Munchkin thinks. All the world a stage for these Americans.

May 9, 1976; Paris

Peter has begun to wear the same Harris tweed jacket every day, the same green crew-neck sweater. His brown hair comes over his white shirt collars now, and he has a bushy mustache.

Each morning from ten to eleven, he sits in the same St.-Germain-des-Prés cafés—Flore, Deux Magots, occasionally Brasserie Lipp. He always drinks *café au lait,* reads the *International Herald-Tribune,* watches the pretty girls like any other American in Paris. Occasionally, he even reads the arrogant diary.

Beside Peter at the café table, Meral Johnson sits and eats half a dozen biscuits with lemon and tea. Antagonist of the Joseph Walthey regime and the Central Intelligence Agency, currently on permanent leave from the San Dominican police force, Johnson exerts a steadying influence on Peter here in France. He is his traveling partner, and his Dutch uncle as well.

According to their latest plan, they'll spend at least the next six months in Europe. In and around Paris . . . down on the Riviera in Nice . . . in Zurich around the Stampfenbachstrasse. Whatever it takes.

Paris is nice in May, Peter thinks as he sips his coffee this particular morning.

It isn't the sunny Caribbean, there's no Jane to share it with him, but Paris is quite acceptable to his way of thinking.

At 10:30 that morning, a hip little Frenchman comes and sits with them at their café table.

"You are the men who look for Carrie Rose?" the Frenchman asks.